Jaunty Jock

and Other Stories

NEIL MUNRO

With an introduction and notes by
Ronnie Renton and
Lesley Bratton

Cover design by Sally Harper, illustrated with details from
'View of Island of Colonsay' by William Smith, and
'The Grassmarket, Edinburgh' by Louise Rayner, reproduced
with permission of Edinburgh Arts

British Library Cataloguing in Publication Data
A catalogue record of this book is available from the British Library

ISBN 1 899863 15 X

First published 1918
This edition published by House of Lochar 1999
based on the text of the Inveraray edition (1935)

The publishers acknowledge subsidy from the Scottish Arts Council
towards the publication of this volume.

THE SCOTTISH ARTS COUNCIL

© Text, Neil Munro, 1999
© Introduction and Notes, Ronnie Renton and Lesley Bratton, 1999

Typeset by XL Publishing Services, Tiverton
Printed in Great Britain
by SRP Ltd, Exeter
for House of Lochar
Isle of Colonsay, Argyll PA61 7YR

Contents

A word of warning from House of Lochar!

Many thanks are due to Ronnie Renton and Leslie Bratton for providing an interesting and informative introduction and additional notes to this collection of Neil Munro's short stories. For your enjoyment, however, we do suggest that, for anyone who would prefer to discover for themselves the 'twist in the tail' of many of the stories, a reading of the introduction is better left until the end of the book!

Introduction

Neil Munro (1863–1930)

NEIL Munro, novelist and journalist, was born in Crombie's Land, Inveraray, Argyll on 3rd June 1863. His mother, Ann Munro, was a kitchen maid, probably in Inveraray Castle. His father has been rumoured to be of the House of Argyll but there is no evidence for this. Soon after his birth Neil's mother took him to live in his grandmother's house in McVicar's Land and it was in this Gaelic-speaking household that he spent most of his childhood.

He received his formal education at Inveraray Parish School which he supplemented with his voracious appetite for books. About 1877 he became a clerk to William Douglas, a local lawyer, but found the work tedious. Like so many other young Highlanders, however, he found no other satisfactory employment locally and so on 1st June 1881 he emigrated to Glasgow where he soon began work as a reporter. After a number of posts with different newspapers he joined the *Glasgow Evening News* with which he was to remain happily for almost the rest of his life.

He made his first mark on the literary scene in 1896 with *The Lost Pibroch and Other Sheiling Stories*, an innovative collection of short stories which seeks to counteract the sentimentality of "Celtic Twilight" writing and to portray the Highlander accurately and in a language which captures Gaelic idiom. In 1897 he reduced his journalistic work considerably to concentrate on literature and in 1898 *John Splendid* was published, a well-judged historical novel of the seventeenth century dealing with the Montrose-Campbell conflict which culminated in the battle of Inverlochy (1645). In 1899 the partly autobiographical *Gilian the Dreamer* appeared, a study of a young boy whose undisciplined sensitivity impedes his ability to act effectively. This was followed by three more novels, *Doom Castle* (1901), *The Shoes of Fortune* (1901) and *Children of Tempest* (1903), all loosely connected with the aftermath of the Jacobite Rising of 1745.

Munro published many humorous sketches in his unsigned column "The Looker On" which appeared every Monday in the *Glasgow Evening News* and, when they later appeared in book form, he adopted for them the *nom de plume* Hugh Foulis. They included stories about the waiter and beadle Erchie MacPherson and the big hearted commercial traveller Jimmy

Swan, but the most celebrated were to be his highly entertaining sketches about the crew of the puffer the *Vital Spark* and their eccentric Captain Para Handy. The first of these appeared in 1905 and Munro continued to produce them for most of his working life. He would have found it ironic that it is for these that he is best remembered today.

After the novel *Children of Tempest* (1903) there is no doubt that Munro felt he had carried the theme of Highland historical romance far enough and turned to the contemporary scene with *The Daft Days* (1907) and *Fancy Farm* (1910). Here he was less successful. In the meantime in 1908 he was honoured with an LL.D. from the University of Glasgow and in 1909 he was made a Freeman of Inveraray.

Not surprisingly, he returned to the historical novel written in "the Highland manner" and in 1914 published his finest work *The New Road*. On one level it is a Highland thriller – the hero Aeneas MacMaster's quest for information about his Jacobite father's mysterious death. At a deeper level, however, like Scott's *Waverley* (1814) it examines the condition of the Highlands and the forces which shape individual destinies. It shows the hero's gradual disillusionment with the romantic glamour of the chiefs as he begins to recognise their vices. Eventually Aeneas comes to understand that only by trade and commerce will the Highlands be "civilised" and the instrument to achieve this will be the New Road Wade is building between Stirling and Inverness. The road becomes a symbol of a more prosperous Gaeldom, but at the same time it will contribute significantly to the permanent destruction of the old Gaelic way of life.

The outbreak of the First World War saw Neil Munro's return to full time journalism. In 1915 his son Hugh was killed in France, near Albert. This trauma coupled with enormous pressure of work – he became editor of the *Evening News* in 1918 – seemed to prevent further large scale literary production. He did, however, publish the collection of witty and sophisticated short stories *Jaunty Jock and Other Stories* (1918), the contents of this volume.

In 1927 Munro's health began to fail and he reluctantly retired from the *Evening News* where he was loved and respected. In October 1930 he received a second LL.D., this time from the University of Edinburgh. Two months later he died at his home, "Cromalt" in Craigendoran, Helensburgh. In 1935 a monument was erected to his memory in Glen Aray. At the dedication ceremony the writer R.B. Cunninghame Graham praised him as "the apostolic successor of Sir Walter Scott".

Munro's literary reputation declined after 1925 when he was accused by Hugh MacDiarmid of writing escapist literature that did not deal with the great national and Highland issues of the day. Modern scholarship, however, shows Munro's critique of Highland life to be much more acute than MacDiarmid had perceived. His literary reputation is being restored to its proper place.

Jaunty Jock and Other Stories (1918)

Neil Munro's short story collection *Jaunty Jock and Other Stories* appeared in 1918. These eleven stories were written over a long period (probably from about 1909) and were gathered for publication towards the end of the First World War. They differ markedly in range, style and content from *The Lost Pibroch and Other Sheiling Stories*, his first collection of stories in "the highland manner" which had marked his arrival on the Scottish literary scene in 1896. They are not all narrowly located in Inveraray and Glen Aray; rather they are spread more widely throughout Scotland – one, indeed, is set in Paris and another in Spain. Furthermore, unusually for Munro, five of them have contemporary settings. There is much less bitterness and blackness in them and many of them are witty and humorous, although one of them, "Young Pennymore", is a beautifully constructed tragedy and may well be Munro's most skilful piece of writing. Overall, the style of this collection is much more sophisticated and diverse.

Of the four comedies in this collection the two longer pieces "Jaunty Jock" and "A Return to Nature" are highly accomplished.

In "Jaunty Jock" Munro himself takes up the challenge which Andrew Lang offered to R.L. Stevenson (and which Stevenson might well have taken up had he lived longer) to write a story which was "to have as its central character Barrisdale, a Highland chief of the eighteenth century whose classical learning and courtly graces in London and Edinburgh were in singular combination with a life of chicane, blackmail and robbery in the Highlands".[1] Indeed, Munro also deals with Barrisdale in his novel *The New Road*,[2] although his treatment in this story is much more light hearted. Here Jaunty Jock is Barrisdale's nickname. He and his cousin are in Edinburgh on legal business when they are given tickets for a masked ball. There, the handsome swashbuckling braggart Barrisdale plays a cruel practical joke on his cousin and a lady. He cunningly pretends to Lord Duthie's daughter that his unhandsome, long-nosed cousin Dan is none other than himself – Barrisdale – and arranges for her to dance with him. When put to the test later in the story, however, Jock shows himself an arrant coward and is suitably humiliated for his bravado when he see the lady's face! The story contains succinct evocations of life in the Edinburgh's Old Town and a brilliant description of the bewildering chaos caused by fire in one of its fourteen storey "lands". Equally interesting is the humorous exploration of the different values held on either side of the Highland line which takes place in the banter between Dan and Lord Duthie's daughter. Concepts like blackmail and *togail* (cattle rustling) that are considered virtues by Highlanders like Barrisdale are the very things that in the Lowlands "we clap men into jyle for".

The comparison of old romantic highland values with the more "civilised" ones of more modern times is again the subject of one of

Munro's wittiest pieces, "A Return to Nature". This story is a comic analogue of Munro's finest novel *The New Road* (1914) where the hero Aeneas MacMaster is cured of his romantic ideas about the Highlands and Highland chieftains and in the end is happy to settle for more "civilised" values of which Wade's New Road itself, built to quell Highland rebellion and to introduce trade and commerce, is the most important symbol.

The hero of "A Return to Nature" is a rather douce and uninspiring lawyer Alexander Macaulay, factor of the island of Kilree. He hears that the owner of the estate and his employer, the Captain of Kilree, is going to demolish the old Macaulay keep of Kincreggan. Consumed by a tremendous rage he lashes out at Kilree with his penknife, wounding him. He then takes off to Kincreggan which he proceeds to fortify and defend in the manner of the ancient clans. Eventually Kilree gets the better of him by flooding him out. He returns home where his wife persuades him to put on his slippers. Immediately he returns to normal and is only too anxious to get back to his legal work.

In the first part of the story Macaulay is the embodiment of the old romantic Highland chieftain: he takes his owner's cattle in a *creach* (cattle raid) and he dons *cuarain* (moccasins) in place of his carpet slippers. He is so successful and attractive that people come from far and near to see Kincreggan and eventually:

> They got a new light upon society and its rights and wrongs, though they might not have the philosophy to explain it clearly; they seemed to see that might was right at any time.

The slippers, however, bring Macaulay to his senses. They correspond to the New Road. Like it they are a symbol of civilisation and "improvement". When the Captain asks Macaulay what broke the spell and learns that the slippers brought him down to earth he says:

> "I wish I had not asked you. I expected a miracle, and you gave me only an epitome of civilisation."

This story satirises the Romantic theory of the Noble Savage. The outrageous behaviour of Macaulay in this story and of Lovat in *The New Road* is no substitute for civilised behaviour. But the line between civilisation and romantic savagery can be very thin.

The other two comic pieces are, by comparison, much slighter but are nonetheless deftly handled. "Copenhagen" is a gently humorous portrait of the whimsical schoolmaster of the little primary school in Glen Aray. A number of his eccentricities are described and then, touchingly, at the end we learn that he wishes to help the war effort in the Crimea by sacrificing his own military pension and he writes a letter to the Admiralty to that effect. The old man's handwriting, however, is so illegible even he cannot read it – but he insists on posting it, so great is his faith in the superior intelligence of the Admiralty to penetrate its illegibility.

"The Tudor Cup" deals with the attempt of two crooked London dealers, Harris and Hirsch, to obtain a silver Tudor cup from the House of Quair near Peebles in the Borders and their discomfiture at the hands of the devious old Sir Gilbert Quair. A similar cup had been sold recently at Sotheby's for £7,000. Amusingly, after Kirsch has persuaded the old guide (none other than the owner, the impoverished Sir Gilbert Quair himself) to lend him the Tudor cup for £1000 so that he can have a copy made of it, it emerges that the Quair cup is itself a copy. Sir Gilbert had sold the original in order to raise funds to pay for the upkeep of his estate! The story concludes on a humorously nationalist note appropriate to its Borders associations, with Sir Gilbert defending his actions in this way:

> "The greed of English thieves brought them here marauding for good six hundred years, and it seems ye're no done yet! My forefolk fought you with the sword, but Gilbert Meldrum Quair must fight you with his wits!"

Another four of the stories in this collection are moral fables, the first two of which can also be classified as fantasy writing.

"The Brooch" is a story in the Hogg tradition set in the Border country in the Covenanting times of the seventeenth century. It is an excellent narrative, one with which Munro himself was especially pleased.[3] It deals with the working out of the punishment of the hero, Wanlock of Manor, by his sister for squandering the money intended for her dowry. She sent him a cursed brooch which she prophesied would bring him

> "Seven shocks of dire disaster and the last the worst."

Once he has the brooch in his possession his fortunes rapidly begin to decline. First of all he loses an expensive lawsuit which reduces him to abject poverty. He then tries to get rid of the brooch but it keeps returning bringing with it six further reversals of fortune, including the death of his son Stephen at the hands of a fierce brownie figure and, finally, his own death when he drinks a goblet of wine in which the brooch itself has been concealed. Too late the maid tries to warn him :

> "The brooch! the brooch!" she screamed: a gleam of comprehension passed for a moment over Wanlock's purpling visage: he raised his arms, and stumbling, fell across the body of his son!

The story gains much of its robust atmosphere from its seventeenth-century Covenanting background with appropriate Biblical reference and its use of lowland folk tradition. Wanlock himself is a Covenanter:

> He cried it [the Holy Name] as they cried it on the moors – his people, when the troopers rode upon them.

but he is not one of the elect:

> Had he not repented? – nay, penitence had been denied him from his very birth, and without repentance well he knew there was no sin's remission. Thus are the unelect at last condemned for a natural inability – terror they have and chagrin at results, but no regret for the essential wrong.

It is this doctrine of predestination wedded to the simple folk idea of the fulfilment of the curse of Wanlock's sister that makes the story so powerful. It emphasises that there can be no escape for the protagonist in this world or the next.

In addition the eerie sound like the bittern's cry which haunts the story adds to the evil atmosphere whilst the brownie-like creature which appears at Wanlock's window and assaults and kills Stephen is drawn from folk tradition. In the story he is compared to the Blednock brownie (Aikendrum in folklore) who was believed to be particularly ugly and, like Wanlock's persecutor, impervious to the influence of the Bible. He also bears great similarity to the leech-like Merodach in James Hogg's story "The Brownie of the Black Haggs". But in Munro's story the brownie is worse than either of these: he is the Accuser of the Brethren himself.

"Isle of Illusion" is a fantasy and a fable which endorses the Greek proverb *meden agan* ("nothing too much"). The hero Morar and his newly-wed wife are spending an idyllic honeymoon cruising round the Outer Isles seeking "for the last pang of pleasure". After some time, however, the bride sees an island on which they have not yet landed and wishes that she and her husband be put ashore there. The Captain is unwilling and warns them against it:

> "Myself, I would not risk it so long as this world has so many pleasant things to be going on with. All I can tell you of Island Faoineas is that, paradise or purgatory, it depends on what one eats and drinks there."

But the girl's will prevails and they spend the night there. In the morning the girl brings Morar berries and immediately after they have eaten them they start to quarrel fiercely. She has a shelister (wild iris) blade in her hand which becomes mysteriously transformed into a poignard and with this in her raging despair she stabs herself. She calls for water and he carries some to her from a stream which had been blessed by a priest from Eriskay. Immediately both are restored to health and love, the couple having learned their lesson.

The story anticipates Barrie's play *Mary Rose* (1924) where local superstition warns Simon not to tempt fate by taking Mary Rose back to the magic island where she disappeared for a time as a child. But "Isle of Illusion" goes further in that it is a modern analogue of the temptation of Adam. When the girl offers Morar the berries he says laughingly:

"The woman tempted me, and I did eat"

and immediately, as in Genesis, the Golden World is shattered and fierce quarrelling breaks out. Redemption comes from the water blessed by a priest, a servant of Christ. In addition, just as he had Wanlock suffer seven disasters in "The Brooch", so in "Isle of Illusion" Munro avails himself of folk tradition to increase the atmosphere of wonder in the story by using the magic number seven to quantify the virtues of the heroine and the number of times the priest blessed the stream. Finally, the name of the island, *Ealan Faoineas*, means more than Munro's translation of it as "Isle of Illusion" would suggest. In Gaelic *Faoineas* has the much stronger meaning of "vanity" or "folly" – of which the young people have to be cured.

"The Scottish Pompadour" is another moral fable, this time set in the Paris of the early nineteenth century. It illustrates the dangers of an indulgent and lavish lifestyle.

Lord Balgowie, the Scottish Pompadour, wishes to see what his own lifestyle looks like from the outside, as it were, and changes places with his secretary who dons his clothes and uses his wealth (but will not indulge in his master's expensive taste in food and prefers a homely diet). His secretary is sought after by leading socialites, including a lady called Mathilde with whom he falls in love. In his idealism he asks her if she would still love him, even if he were poor. Her witty reply shatters him:

"*Farceur!*" said she, "now you are romantic, and to talk romance in seriousness is ridiculous."
Of a sudden he saw her what she really was – vain, cruel, calculating, parched in soul, despite her saintly face.

Just as the truth about the selfishness of human nature is dawning on his innocence his mother, from whom he had learned his straightforward decency, arrives to save him from any blunder he might make. She had jaloused from his letters that the girl he was in love with was calculating and insincere. And, ironically, Lord Balgowie, the libertine who was watching his own lifestyle enacted before him by his secretary has become a morality figure, feared by the socialites:

"... he looks – more like a conscience than a human secretary!... Get rid of him – get rid of him!"

This story parodies the lad o' pairts tradition. The highly educated young man of humble background does *not* go on to great things in French society and presumably returns to his roots, but his kailyard values – "a homely taste in viands, and his honest heart" – triumph and teach his master the folly of his ways.

"The First-foot" is a humorous moral tale. It is Hogmanay. A dissolute young man, Black Andy, has drunk away all his money and is now reluctantly returning home to face the music. It is a fiercely stormy night and Andy finally comes to a remote little inn where he seeks shelter for the night. The landlady is decidedly unwelcoming. Her husband is much more genial and warm, especially when he hears the nature of the young man's security:

"But what's your security?" demanded madam, and the goodman sighed...
"God," said he...
"Ye couldna hae better!" cried the innkeeper, and drawing a chopin of ale for the pious gentleman, beat down by the very gust of his geniality the rising opposition of the woman's manner.

In his room Andy discovers a bag of cash belonging to the wife which he rightly deduces the husband knows nothing of. He steals this and flees out into the wild night. However, he gets lost on Flanders Moss and ironically finds himself back at the self same inn. There he "pays the lawin'" to the wife with the stolen guineas.

Divine Providence, then, ensures that Andy puts his wrong to right, that the wife is punished for her bad-tempered lack of hospitality and for deceiving her husband about the existence of her fortune by being temporarily separated from it and, most important, that the genial, apparently ingenuous innkeeper's faith in God is justified. He was in no doubt that Andy would be a "good risk" because

"I kent ye had Grand Security."

The three remaining stories are of quite disparate types. "The Silver Drum" is a romantic story of war, love and mistaken identity and the author displays a sure use of flashback technique. The narrative moves from a contemporary discussion in an Edinburgh studio between the narrator and a sculptor, back to the sack of Ciudad Rodrigo during the

Napoleonic/Peninsular War. The story, however, is flawed by too heavy a reliance on coincidence which makes this piece the least successful of the volume. It is at its best when describing events in war-torn Spain.

"The Tale of the Boon Companion" returns to the style of the early *The Lost Pibroch and Other Sheiling Stories* collection of 1896. It purports to be a folktale and is set at the same time as the novel *John Splendid*, the period of the sack of Inveraray by Alasdair MacColla immediately before the Battle of Inverlochy in 1645. The setting, like *The Lost Pibroch* stories, is again very precisely the Inveraray area and in particular Glen Shira. The farms of Maam and Stuckgoy are mentioned as well as Ben Shean and Ben Bhuidhe. Also like many of the early stories this story's springboard is a proverb:

"Every man his boon companion, every man his maid."

The main character of the tale, Red John, is in the mould of John Splendid and Jaunty Jock. He is a man of the easy word, a flatterer, a great teller of tales and singer of songs, but rootless and unreliable – yet for all that great company and well-intentioned:

"I'm foe to none, woman," he cried, "except perhaps to a man they call Red John, and the worst enemy ever I had was welcome to share the last penny in my sporran. I have my weakness, I'll allow, but my worst is that my promise is better than my performance, and my most ill-judged acts are well intended."

He becomes very friendly with Alan whose sweetheart Ealasaid grows very resentful of the increasing amount of time they spend together to her neglect until she eventually accuses him of wrecking people's lives:

"You're like the weak man in the *ceilidh* story," pressed the girl.
"How?" quo' he.
"Because you botch life," said she. "Let a girl tell it you. And the pity of it is you'll do it in the end."

The second part of the story deals with Red John's reparation for his self-ishness. There is an attack on Ealasaid's home in Glen Shira by Colkitto's men and he seeks to rescue her and save the lovers. But for all his brave intentions he "botches" the attempt and the story ends in tragic irony when he inadvertently sends them to their death.

Finally, "Young Pennymore" is a taut and grimly ironic story of mistaken identity. It deals with the trial and execution of a young Jacobite, John Clerk of Pennymore, for being art and part in the murder of Campbell of Clonary. Clearly inspired, like Stevenson's *Kidnapped*, by the infamous

Appin murder, it is set very precisely on 5th September 1752. (There is a significant parallel with Stevenson's *Kidnapped* in that both Campbell of Lochgair in this story and Colin Campbell, the Red Fox, in *Kidnapped* are murdered as a result of being distracted on their journeys and then shot by a hidden assailant.)

The story is in three movements. It opens with a short but dramatic trial scene in which John Clerk is condemned to die. This is followed by a description of his parents frantically attempting to enlist the help of influential people to plead on his behalf and the mother is eventually successful in obtaining the help of Campbell of Lochgair who goes off to Edinburgh to petition the Lord Advocate. When Lochgair fails to appear by the day before the execution the parents leave in the pitch dark of the following stormy morning to visit their son in Inveraray where he is in jail. The mother fondles a gun in her plaid. But the cart breaks down and they are stranded at the foot of the gallows just outside the town. The wife, in her anger, assumes that the body hanging there is her son. They cut the body down and put it in the cart.

The third movement tells of the journey home in which the woman viciously blames Campbell of Lochgair for not intervening. Suddenly they hear his horse galloping towards the town. The woman prepares to shoot him but her husband finally manages to wrest the gun from her. She cruelly goads him into firing at Lochgair. Momentarily enraged he pulls the trigger and Lochgair dies. When, however, they have disposed of his body and gone through all his papers they discover that Lochgair had indeed brought the reprieve for John and was clearly in haste to deliver it. They then go to the cart and pull the plaid off the body to discover that it was not their son!

This story is taut, tense and beautifully constructed. The mother's pride (*hubris*) is the driving force of the action. The woman does not want to be seen in the town lest she become an object of pity and she does not want her son to have the indignity of a public execution, so they go to the town in the dark of early morning. Her intention is to deliver to him his gun so that he can take his own life. The repeated reference to this gun which she fondles underneath her plaid becomes a motif in itself and increases the atmosphere of menace throughout the tale. Furthermore, because she is disposed to think the worst, the mother imagines that the body on the gibbet must be her son and so her imagining becomes her sadly mistaken reality.

The husband, on the other hand, is a peaceable and holy person who strives to keep his wife's anger in check but, temporarily unhinged by the news that Lochgair was the true father of his son, now becomes the instrument of her vengeance. In his innocence he had actually believed that the changes involved by the implementation of the Gregorian Calendar (since technically 5th September did not exist) might have saved his son – but now any hope from that quarter is past.

The most appalling irony of all is that at the end of the story John Clerk is still alive, the reprieve is actually in their possession – the boy's own father had brought it! – but now that Lochgair has been murdered, his body flung into the sea and his other possessions destroyed, what can be done to save John? Had the woman left well alone and trusted Lochgair all would have been well!

Jaunty Jock and Other Stories (1918), whilst maintaining a strong link with *The Lost Pibroch and Other Sheiling Stories* through "The Tale of the Boon Companion", shows considerable development in the author's handling of the short story genre since that early publication of 1896. As always Munro's description of place and atmosphere is beautifully judged but this collection shows more balance and sophistication. There is a greater variety of approach and setting and some very interesting experimentation with the fable and, as one would expect from the creator of Para Handy, the comic mode. We also have one superbly constructed tragedy. All of the stories in this collection show the craftsmanship of the true professional writer but "Jaunty Jock", "A Return to Nature", "The Brooch" and "Young Pennymore" stand out as masterpieces. They confirm Hugh MacDiarmid's judgement in the *Scottish Educational Journal*, 3rd July 1925 (whatever his reservations about the rest of Munro's fiction) that

> Neil Munro remains, on the whole, one of the six best short story writers Scotland has yet produced, the others being R.L.Stevenson, "Fiona Macleod", John Buchan, R.B. Cunninghame Graham, and (to count them as one) the Findlater sisters.

Notes

1 Neil Munro, *The Looker-On*, Edinburgh, 1933: p288
2 Neil Munro, *The New Road*, Edinburgh, 1994: Chs 8&9, pp76–94
3 "'The Brooch' may be a little too sombre for some tastes, but I am more than satisfied with it technically than with any short story I have written. It is, if anything, perhaps a little too crowded and close in the texture, however." Letter from Neil Munro to George Blackwood, 3rd December1909.

(Further details on the life and work of Neil Munro can be obtained in the introduction to Neil Munro, The Lost Pibroch and Other Sheiling Stories, *House of Lochar, Colonsay, 1996.)*

Jaunty Jock

Chapter I: THE WEST BOW BALL

THE last of the West Bow balls before Lady Charlotte ran away with her dancing-master was on a dirty evening in November. Edinburgh was all day wrapped in haar, and now came rain that made the gutters run like mountain burns and overflow into the closes, to fall in shallow cataracts to the plain below. There was a lively trade in the taverns. "Lord! there's a sneezer for ye!" said the customers ordering in their ale, not really minding the weather much, for it was usual and gave a good excuse for more assiduous scourging of the nine-gallon tree; but their wives, spanging awkwardly on pattens through the mud on their way to the fishwife at the Luckenbooths for the supper haddocks, had such a breeze in their petticoats and plaids they were in a terror that they should be blown away upon the blasts that came up the gulleys between the towering "lands," and daring slates and chimney-pots, and the hazards of emptied vessels from the flats above, kept close to the wall as luggers scrape the shore of Fife when the gale's nor'-west.

Lady Charlotte was director of the dance – a creature most majestic, who ballooned about the room as if not her feet but her big hooped petticoat conveyed her, the only woman without a mask; that in her office would be useless. All the other women kept theirs on, with silken cords bit between the teeth (except when a favourite partner caused a titter). Below the velvet, when it tilted up, they showed the cheeks of youth and beauty, sometimes a little high in the bone for classic taste, and a patch on the chin just at the point where to a resolute lad it looked like a defiance. The flute, the hautbois, and the 'cello gave body to the melody of the harpsichord, somewhat flat the whole of them, for the place was sweltering, and the stuccoed ceiling sweated, and the walls.

A gentleman, conspicuous from the fact that he wore no wig, stood in the dusk at the foot of the room, away from the guttering candelabra, and put up his hand to hide a yawn. The minuet was beyond him, and seemed to him who came from the wilds, where the languid had no place in merriment, a somewhat insipid affair. In the cardroom, where old dowagers played cards till their girls should be ready to go home, and the young ones sat with their chosen gallants, sipping tea in the latest manner, he had

1

ventured a harmless remark to a lady neither too young nor too lovely to resent a politeness at a masque assembly, and she had fled to her friends as if he were an ogre.

He was neither surprised nor vexed; he was accustomed to have the fair avoid him, though scarcely with such obvious fastidiousness as to-night. It was one of the things to be expected by a man with a crooked nose and the plainness of his other features in conformity with that one, even if he had not happened to be there incognito.

"To the devil!" said he to himself. "I cannot expect them to be civil to any casual Jo at a two-and-sixpenny ball." And he yawned again, impatient for the coming away of his cousin, whose gallantries to a lady at the other end of the room seemed unending. From that cousin he neither expected the ordinary courtesies of life nor desired them. They were usually as cool to each other as if they had sprung from different clans, and it was only the accident of a law plea affecting the family in its various branches that brought them privately to the capital and to the same lodgings from widely different parts of their native shire, and from widely different ways of life.

Whatever the cousin had to say to madam, she was pretty merry on the head of it, and seemed entranced with her gallant. He was such a coxcomb surely as never before came off the heather, with his Genoa velvet coat, his sky-blue breeches, and a waistcoat of the tartan of his clan, a thin, delicate, lady-like sword at his haunch that better knew the swing of the claymore.

"A rogue, Jock! and a tongue to wile the bird off the tree," thought the man with the crooked nose, in no envy at all, but just in a distaste at nature's perversity; and he saw that his cousin and the lady looked at him as if he were the object of their conversation.

To his astonishment, the lady, at the forming of the next quadrille, was brought to him by Lady Charlotte. "You see, if the mountain'll not come to Mahomet, Mahomet maun just come to the mountain," said the directress airily. "Here's a leddy I'm determined shall not miss her quadrille, and you are very lucky, Mr – Mr – "

"Macdonald," said he, with a bow and a glance of shrewdness at the young lady, who had plainly made the arrangements herself for the introduction.

"Mr Macdonald – just so! a rale decent clan," said Lady Charlotte, who prided herself upon the quality of her Scots. "I mind you had the tickets from Lord Duthie; you're lucky to have the chance of the bonniest partner in the room."

"I'll take your word for it," said he, with another glance at a very soothfast mask that came down on as sweet a pair of lips as ever man took craving for.

At a quadrille he was not amiss if one could get over the crook in his nose and the rugged plainness of his countenance generally. When he was done and brought the lady to a seat, she was good enough to say he danced divinely. She had herself the carriage of a swan, her voice was of a ravishing and caressing quality, with none of the harsh, high-pitched, East-country accent that would have grated on Macdonald's ears, and yet there was something shallow in her phrase and sentiment.

"You are very good to say so, ma'am. I rarely dance, and I have seldom danced less at an assembly than I have done to-night," said he, taking the compliment at its real value, for his dancing was a point on which he had no illusions.

The lady toyed with her fan; her eyes, mischievous and profound as wells and of the hue of plums, sparkled through the holes in her mask.

"Oh la! and you divine at it, I declare! Our Edinburgh belles, then, do not tempt you, Mr Macdonald? But I daresay you will think them quite good enough for our Edinburgh beaux; now, did you ever in your life see such gawks?"

Macdonald rubbed his chin. "On the contrary," said he, "I was just thinking them uncommon spruce and handsome."

"You are very tolerant; have you any other virtues to be aired?" said the lady with a smile that puzzled him. "There's still another dance, I see; her ladyship is fairly in the key to-night; you'll have time to tell me all of them seriatim, missing out the lesser ones *brevitatis causa.*"

"H'm!" thought he; "her father's in the law," and wondered who she was. "I could tell you all of them in the time it would take to dance a step of the Highland Fling," said he.

"Faith, there's modesty! Item, Mr Macdonald?" and she sat back in her chair, her hoops bulged out in front of her like the bastion of a fort.

He counted them on his fingers humorously. "Item, the tolerance you have given me credit for, though you have no example of it as yet, madam; item, an honest liking for my fellows, even the scamps of them; item, a habit of aye paying my way; item – " his forefinger hovered dubiously over the other hand, but never lighted on another virtue. "I declare to you I have got to the end of my list and the man has not yet finished the tuning of his fiddle," he said, laughing in a way so pleasant it almost made amends for his unhappy nose.

He had taken a seat beside her, she tapped him with her fan upon the knees with an air of the superior that struck him as a little droll, and, looking straight in his face, said in an affected Scots, as if to take the sting from the words: "A' very fine, Maister Macdonald, a' very fine! What have ye given me here but twa-three virtues that come – except maybe the last – so easy to maist folk they're nae mair to your credit than that you should sup kail wi' a spoon?"

"A poor show, I confess it, ma'am; if you want a list of more brilliant virtues, you should try my worthy cousin, your last partner," he replied.

"Do you tell me that – Barrisdale?" said the lady, burring her "r's" with a gusto to make him certain she had no dubiety regarding his identity.

He could not hide a little start of surprise, for he thought the secret of his cousin and himself being in Edinburgh was known to but two men there, Lord Duthie and Mackee.

"You're the daughter of Lord Duthie," said he, remembering her law Latinity.

She was confused at so shrewd a guess, but admitted he was right. "It has long been my wish," said she, "to have a crack with a Highland rob –, with a Highland person of your experience; and I must confess I asked Lady Charlotte for the introduction, though you may not think it modest. Let me tell you that I'm disappointed; it ill becomes a gentleman of Barrisdale's reputation to be claiming such paltry common virtues as those you have named to charm the ear of an unknown lady in a mask. They credit ye with Latin and French, and say ye cut a dash whiles in London – oh la! a wonnerfu' man entirely! – but upon my word, I never thought to get a catechist in my Hielan cateran."

"Here's a comedy," thought he, looking across the room to his cousin. "How in the world did you discover me?" he asked her; "did my cousin –"

"He did," said she, "and he told me not to mention it; but you see, I take the privilege of my sex."

"I cannot but be flattered at your interest, ma'am, I'm sure, and I hope you will not let the thing go further so long as I'm in Edinburgh. Now that I'm discovered, I'm wae to be back to my ruffian gang," said he, with a quizzing air. "I must have a most tremendous reputation, and I would not wonder if you could go over all my history."

"I daresay I know the worst of it."

"Do you? Faith! it's more than I do myself; might I ask you to be jogging my memory?"

"When I come to think of it," said she, "the very virtues that you claim are what in the rough bounds of the Hielans may well manifest themselves in fashions that hereabouts in lalland towns we clap men into jyle for."

"Indeed, I should not wonder, ma'am," said he; "what's counted a crime in one parish, even in the Hielans, is often looked on as a Christian act in others not a glen removed."

"You talk of tolerance, Barrisdale; was it that made you hide in Ben Alder for a twelvemonth the man that shot Breadalbane's factor?"

"He was a very old man, the factor, Miss Duthie," said he glibly. "He would have died in another winter, anyway, by all appearances, and not half so handsomely as with a bullet. And the poor fellow who shot him – you would not have us send a man with a wife and ten of a family to the gallows?"

"Lord!" cried the lady, affecting to be out of patience. "You are a rebel too, my father tells me, and all for having back those Papist Stuarts and putting the dear King away out of the country. Is that a sample of your love for your fellow-men?"

4

"Logic," thought Macdonald, "is not a branch that's taught with the virginals and tambouring in lawyers' families." "Well, ma'am," said he, "could you blame me? I have been in France a while myself, and I ken the kind of drink they have to drink there; I would not poison dogs with it. I would have Jamie back for no other reason than to save what relics of his stomach may be to the fore. What's that but love for my fellows?"

"Was it that made you fight with the London gentleman and send him – poor soul – to his Maker at five o'clock on a cold winter morning?"

"It's a small world. Who would have thought the gossip of that trivial affair would have travelled to an Edinburgh assembly? Sure you would not have had me put off the occasion till the summer weather; we were both warm enough at the time, I assure you, or that black folly they call a duel had never been engaged in."

"You have the name of – of – I hate to mention it," said the lady, now grown eager and biting her under lip.

"Oh, out with it! out with it! Crown Counsel should never be blate, ma'am; on my word, the talent for cross-examination would seem to run in the family."

"Blackmail and – " said she in a whisper.

"One at a time!" said Macdonald. "That's the prose way of putting it; up north we put it differently. You call it robbery; we call it rent. Some charge the rent by the penny-land or the acre; we charge it by the sound night's sleep, and the man who rents immunity for his cattle from Barrisdale gets as good value for his money as the man who rents some acres of dirt from Appin."

Madam worked her fan industriously – now she was on his heels, and could not spare so plain a mercenary. "You steal cattle," was her next charge.

"Steal! ma'am," said Barrisdale, with a frown. "It is not the bonniest word; up north we call it *togail* – lifting. It is an odd world, mistress, and every man of us has to do some sort of lifting for a living – if not in the glen, then in the market-place, where the act is covered in a fine confusion. If we lift a *creach* now and then in Barrisdale there are other clans that lift from us, and at the season's end no one is much the worse, and there has been much frolic and diversion."

"On the same reasoning, then, you would justify the attempt at abducting Glen Nant's rich daughter?" said the lady.

"Do you happen to have seen her?"

"I have," said the lady, and could not for her life have kept from smiling. "It was the sight of her spoiled what small romantics I had about the Hielan cateran."

"Are you sure there are none to the fore yet?"

"Not a morsel!" said the lady, looking point-blank at his nose.

"*Mo thruagh!*" said Macdonald tragically; "then are we indeed forsaken."

"You made a shabby flight, by all accounts, from the lady's brother."

"Humph!" said he, for the first time disconcerted; indeed, it was a story no way creditable to Clan Macdonald. "I think," said he, "we'll better let that flea stick to the wall," and looked across the room to where his cousin sat glowering in a manifest anxiety.

"Oh, Barrisdale, Barrisdale, can ye no' be a good man?" said Miss Duthie, in a petty lady-like concern, and unable to keep her eyes from that unlucky nose.

He put up his hand and covered it. She flushed to the neck that he should so easily have divined her, and he laughed.

"It's no use trying, ma'am," said he. "Let me be as good as gold and I would never get credit for it from your sex, that must always fancy that a handsome face never goes but with a handsome heart."

She rose with an air of vexation to leave him, very red below her mask; the last dance was on the point of ending, the dowagers were coming in with their Paisley plaids on their shoulders. "I would never hurt any person's feelings by allusion to his personal appearance," she said, as she was turning away.

"I am sure of it, ma'am," said he; "you are most considerate."

Chapter II: THE FIRE

Macdonald and his cousin Jock walked to their lodging in Halkerston's Wynd without a lanthorn. The watch cried, "Twal o'clock, twal o'clock, and a perishin' cauld nicht"; they could hear the splash of his shoes in the puddles of the lane although they could not see him. The town now rose above the haar that brooded in the swampy hollow underneath the citadel; the rain was gone, the stars were clear, the wind moaned in the lanes and whistled on the steep. It was like as they were in some wizard fortress cut from rock, walking in mirk ravines, the enormous houses dizzy overhanging them, the closes running to the plains on either hand in sombre gashes. Before them went sedans and swinging lanterns and flambeaux that left in their wake an odour of tow and rosin not in its way unpleasant.

"Yon was a dubious prank upon the lady," said Macdonald, and his cousin laughed uproariously.

"Upon my word, Donald," said he, "I could not for the life of me resist it. I declare it was better than a play; I have paid good money for worse at a play."

"And still and on a roguish thing," said Macdonald, hastening his step. "You were aye the rogue, Jaunty Jock."

"And you were aye the dullard, Dismal Dan," retorted the other in no bad humour at the accusation. "To be dull is, maybe, worse. You had the opportunity – I risked that – to betray me if you liked."

"You knew very well I would not do that."

"Well, I thought not, and if you did not take the chance to clear yourself when you got it, there's no one but yourself to blame. Here was madam – quite romantical about the Highlands, as I found at our first country dance, and languishing to see this Barrisdale that she has heard from some one – (who the devil knows? that beats me) – was to be at Lady Charlotte's ball. 'I'm sorry to say he's my own cousin,' says I – 'a Hielan cousin, it does not count when rogues are in the family.' 'You must point him out to me,' said she. I gave her three guesses to pick out the likeliest in the room, and she took you at the first shot."

"A most discerning young person!" said Macdonald.

"She knew your history like a sennachie, lad, and rogue as she made you, I believe she would have forgiven you all but for that nose of yours."

"Oh, damn my nose!" cried Macdonald. "It's not so very different from the common type of noses."

"Just that! just that! not very different, but still a little skew. Lord! man, you cannot expect to have all the graces as well as all the virtues. Madam picked you out at all events, and I was not in the key to contradict her. She paid you (or was it me?) the compliment of saying you were not at all like her idea of a man with the repute of Barrisdale."

"Very likely! Indeed, I could guess she was more put out at that than at finding herself speaking to a scamp who laughed at his own misdeeds. You made a false move; Jock, had you admitted you were the man, she would not have been greatly mortified. In any case, she thought to improve the occasion with advice. She told me to be good!"

Barrisdale could hardly speak for laughing. "You kept up the play at any rate," said he, "for when I saw her to her chair, ' Yon's an awful man, your cousin,' said she. What do you think of her?"

"Something of a simpleton, something of a sentimentalist, and a very bonny face forbye to judge by her chin – that was all of it I saw."

"She kept too tight a mask for even me to see her face. Man, ye've missed her chief charm – she has twa thousand a year of her own. I had it from herself, so you see I'm pretty far ben. With half a chance I could make a runaway match of it; I'm sure I took her fancy."

"Tuts! Jock. I thought you had enough of runaway matches; take care she has not got a brother," said Macdonald.

Jaunty Jock scowled in the dark, but made no answer.

Their lodging was in a land deep down in the Wynd. Flat on flat it rose for fourteen stories, poverty in its dunnies (as they called its cellars), poverty in its attics, and between the two extremes the wonderfullest variety of households bien or wealthy – the homes of writers, clerks, ministers, shopkeepers, tradesmen, gentlemen reduced, a countess, and a judge – for there, though the Macdonalds did not know, dwelt Lord Duthie with his daughter. In daytime the traffic of the steep scale stair went like the road to a fair, at night the passages were black and still as vaults. "A fine place the town, no doubt," said Jaunty Jock, "but, lord, give me the hills for it!"

They slept in different rooms. The morning was still young when one of them was wakened by the most appalling uproar on the stair. He rose and saw his window glowing; he looked from it, and over on the gables of the farther land he saw the dance of light from a fire. He wakened Jaunty Jock. "Get up," said he, "the tenement's in blazes." They dressed in a hurry, and found that every one in the house but themselves had fled already. The door stood open; on the landing crushed the tenants from the flats above, men and women in a state of horror, fighting like brutes for their safety. The staircase rang with cries – the sobbing of women, the whimper of bairns, and at the foot a doorway jammed. Frantic to find themselves caught like rats, and the sound of the crackling fire behind them, the trapped ones elbowed and tore for escape, and only the narrowness of the passage kept the weaker ones from being trampled underfoot. All this Macdonald could define only by the evidence of his ears, for the stair was wholly in pitch darkness.

"By God! we'll burn alive!" said Jaunty Jock, every shred of his manhood gone, and trembling like a leaf. Their door was in a lobby recessed from the landing – an eddy wherein some folk almost naked drifted weeping to find themselves helpless of getting farther. "Where's the fire?" asked Macdonald from one of them, and had to shake him before he got an answer.

"Two landings farther up," said the fellow, "in Lord Duthie's flat."

"Lord Duthie's flat!" cried Macdonald; "and is he safe?"

"He's never hame yet; at least, I never heard him skliffin' on the stair, but his dochter cam' back hersel' frae the assembly."

"Is she safe?" asked Macdonald.

"Wha' kens that?" replied the man, and threw himself into the stair, the more able now to fight because of his rest in the eddy.

"It looks gey bad for your runaway match, Jock," said Macdonald. "Here's a parcel of the most arrant cowards. My God, what a thin skin of custom lies between the burgess and the brute beast. That poor lass! It's for you and me, Jock, to go up and see that she's in no greater danger than the rest of us."

He spoke to deaf ears, for Jock was already fighting for his place among the crowd. His cousin did the same, but with another purpose: his object was to scale the stair. He pushed against the pressure of the panic, mountains were on his shoulders, and his ribs were squeezed into his body as if with falling rocks. His clothes were torn from his back, he lost his shoes, and a frantic woman struck him on the face with the heavy key of her door that with a housewife's carefulness she treasured even when the door it was meant for was burned, and the blood streamed into his eyes.

He was still in the dark of the stair; the fire at least was not close enough to stop his mounting, so up he felt his way in a hurry till he reached Lord Duthie's flat. A lobby that led to the left from the landing roared with flame that scorched him; a lobby on the right was still untouched. He hammered at the only shut door but got no answer, plied the risp as well with the same result, then threw it in with a drive of the shoulders. He gave a cry in the entrance and, getting no response, started to go through the rooms. At the third the lady sat up in her bed and cried at the intruder. "The land's on fire, ma'am," said he quietly in the dark.

"Fire!" she cried in horror. "Oh, what shall I do? Who are you?"

"Barrisdale," said he, remembering his rôle and determined to make this his last appearance in it. "You have plenty of time to dress, and I'll wait for you on the landing."

He went out with a sudden project in his mind, ran down the stair with its litter of rags and footwear and found it almost vacant, the obstruction at the bottom being cleared. "Take your time, my friends," said he, "there's not the slightest danger; the fire will not get this length for half an hour yet."

His cousin came back from the crush. "As sure's death, I'm glad to see you and sorry I never bided," said he. "You never came on her; I knew very well she must have got out at the outset."

"Indeed!" said Barrisdale. "As it happens, she's yonder yet, and I had the honour to wake her; I fancy she's taking her hair from the curl-papers at this moment. You never had a better chance of getting credit for a fine action very cheaply. It was in the dark I wakened her; I told her I was Barrisdale and would return when she was dressed. You may go back to her."

"Man, I wouldn't mind," said the cousin; "but what's the object?" he added suspiciously.

"Only that I'm tired of being Barrisdale to suit you. If you like to be Barrisdale and carry your own reputation, you'll have the name of saving her life – one thing at least to your credit that'll maybe make her forget the rest. With a creature so romantical, I would not wonder if it came to the runaway match after all."

"Faith, I'll risk it," said Jaunty Jock, and ran up the stair. He came down with the lady on his arm, and took her to a neighbour's.

"And did you confess to your identity?" asked his cousin when they met again.

"I did," he answered gloomily.

"Surely she did not boggle at the Barrisdale; I was certain it would make little odds to a lady of her character."

"Oh, she was willing enough, but it's not a match," said Jaunty Jock. "After this, I'll always see the mask off first; she had a worse nose than yourself!"

Young Pennymore

OF the half-dozen men of Mid-Argyll condemned on one account or another for their part in the Rebellion, the last, and the least deserving of so scurvy a fate, was young John Clerk of Pennymore. He had been out in the affair more for the fun of the thing than from any high passion of politics; he would have fought as readily for the Duke as for the Young Pretender if the Duke had appealed to him first; he was a likeable lad to all who knew him, and the apple of his mother's eye.

The hanging of young John Clerk seemed at the time all the more harsh a measure since he was not charged directly with rebellion, but with being actor or art and part in the death of the Captain of Clonary, who was shot on his way from Culloden by a gang of lurking Jacobites of whom the lad was one, and maybe innocent. The murderers scattered to the mist and to the sea. For six years Clerk sequestered in the land of France, and was caught at last in a tender filial hour when he had ventured home to see his folk. A squad of the Campbells found him skulking in the wood of Pennymore on the very afternoon of his return; he had not even had the time to see his people, and the trinkets and sweetmeats he had meant for his mother were strewn from his pockets among the bracken as he was being dragged before the Lords.

They looked at him – these dour and exigent gentlemen – with eyes that held no pity, not men at all for the nonce, but bowelless, inexorable legal mechanism; and Elchies, squeaking like a showman at a fair, sentenced him to the gallows.

"John Clerk," he said, "you have had an impartial trial; you have been defended by an able advocate, who has made the most of a wretched cause; the jury has found you guilty as libelled, and it only rests with this court to pronounce sentence accordingly. You may yet, during the brief period you have to live, best serve your country and your friends by warning them against those pernicious principles which have brought you to this untimely end, and may the Lord have mercy on your soul!"

Then the doomster declared doom – that young John Clerk be handed over to the Sheriff-Depute, hanged by the neck on the burgh gibbet at Creag-nan-caoraich on the 5th September, and thereafter left for a time in chains.

The lad made a bow to his judges, gave a last quick, eager glance about the court to assure himself his parents were not there, and then he was hurried down the trap-door to the cells.

.   .   .

There was still a month to go before the day of execution, and the Clerks of Pennymore – the proud and bitter dame and her pious husband – scoured the shire in search of sympathetic gentlemen of influence, and forswore sleep itself in their efforts to secure reprieve. They seemed, poor souls! miraculous in their great endurance, singly or together tramping here and there on a quest no neighbour dared to share, tragic to see upon the highway, horrible to hear at midnight when their cart went rumbling through the sleeping clachans. Sympathy was plentiful, but influence was shy, and the hopes of Pennymore were narrowed at last to Campbell of Lochgair, a lawyer himself, with the ear of His Grace and the Crown authorities.

Lochgair, more, as it strangely seemed, for the sake of the peevish dame than for her husband's, promised his active interest, and almost guaranteed release, and in the latter days of August went to Edinburgh to wait on the Lord Advocate, who was Prestongrange. It was the year of the stunted corn – 1752 – and never in the memory of man had been such inclement weather. The seas would seem to have forgotten the ways of peace; the glens were flooded, and the Highlands for a space were cut off from the Lowland world, and in a dreary privacy of storm. So the days passed – for most folk as if Time itself were bogged among the mire – for the man and wife in Pennymore as the flap of wings. They longed each evening for the morrow since it might bring welcome news, and yet they grudged the night and looked with terror on the dawn, since it brought the horrid hour a vigil closer.

And there were no tidings from Lochgair!

"I might have known! I might have known! – a traitor ever, like his clan!" cried the mother, all her patience drained to the bitter dregs, wringing her hands till the blood came to the knuckles. "Lochgair will see the laddie hanged, and never jee his beaver. Too well I know his promises! We're here forgot, the pair of us, and all the world sleeping sound, no way put about at the thought of young John Clerk. Deserted of men! deserted of men!" and her cry rose like a dirge in their lonely dwelling.

"But not of God and His grace," said her husband, shrinking before the fury of her eye. "I have trusted Lochgair in this with all my heart, and he cannot betray us. He knows that his breath is all that lies between our laddie and eternity."

"Oh, trust!" she hissed. "I ken the man; but I have trusted too, this fortnight, till my very heart is rent, yet God Himself cannot put off the 5th September."

"Yea, even that, if it be His will; our times are in His hands," said the pious husband, and turned him again to his Bible. But the woman's doubts were justified, and on the morning of the day before their son should perish, they yoked the horse and drove in the cart to the burgh town to see him for the first time in the cell he had shared with some doomed sheep-stealers.

Six miles lay between their home and the tolbooth gates, and yet it was in pitch-black night they came to the confines of the burgh, for they dreaded the pitying eyes of men and women. And all the way the woman fondled something in her plaid. They saw, afar, and few, and melancholy, wan lights in the burgh lands, blurred by the weeping rain; and at this spectacle – which told them the world went on its ordinary way and thought of breakfast, while their lad sat counting the hours, and they were engaged with misery – the man put his hand on the woman's shoulder with a grip of steel, and she gave the last sob that was ever heard from her. For ever after she was a woman made of stone. The horse, as if it shared their feeling, stopped on the highway, reared itself in terror of something unseen, and snapped its belly-band, and the cart stood still under heaving beeches whose windy branches filled the dark with noise and cried down the very waves which roared on Creag-nan-caoraich.

The man jumped from the cart and fumbled with the harness, to find that further progress, wanting a girth, was not to be contemplated.

"I will walk into the town," he said, "and get a rope, if you sit here till I return. You will not mind my leaving you, Margaret?"

"Mind!" she exclaimed with bitterness; "I have learned my lesson, and there is no more to mind." But she fondled the thing concealed in her plaid, and her man walked quickly towards the wan lights of the tenements, leaving her all alone.

For a moment only she heard his footsteps, the sound of them soon lost in the din of nature – the uproar of the forest trees, whose ponderous branches creaked; the wind, canorous, blowing between the mountains; the booming crepitation of the sea upon the rocks. And yet no sense of solitude depressed her, for her mind was occupied by one triumphant thought – that young John Clerk should at least be spared the horror and shame of a public execution.

She had drawn, at first, the drenched plaid over her head to shield her and shut her in from the noise of tempest; but her hands in a little while were so busily engaged with her secret possession that the tartan screen at last rolled back on her shoulders, and she was aware of another sound than those of nature – the near, faint clang of chains. It was scarcely audible, but unmistakable – the beat of a loose end of iron links against wood, somewhere above her head, as she sat in the cart by the side of Creag-nan-caoraich. She stared up into the darkness and saw nothing, then stood to her feet and felt above her with trembling hand.

Her fingers searchd along a beam with a rope attached to it, whose

12

meaning flooded to her brain with a gush that stunned; she touched a dead man's feet! and the pitiless clouds that had swept all night across the heavens heaved for a moment from the face of the reeling moon, and she saw the wretch upon the gibbet!

"My son! my son!" she screamed till the rocks and trees gave back the echo, and yet the distant lights of the burgh town glowed on with unconcern.

.   .   .

Her cries had ceased; she was sunk in a listless torpor in the bottom of the cart when her man returned in a state as wretched as her own, running with stumbling feet along the rutted highway.

"My God! my God!" said he, "I have learned of something dreadful!"

"I have learned it for myself," said his wife. "You're a day behind the fair."

"Not one day, but eleven of them," said her husband, hardly taking her meaning. "It is the fifteenth of September, and I'm so fearful of the worst. I dared not rap at a door in the town and ask."

"The fifteenth of September," she repeated dully; "we have not slept so sound this month back that we could miss a fortnight. Have you lost your reason?"

"I have seen a placard put up on the mercat cross," said her husband, with his brow upon the horse's back. "I read it in the light of the tolbooth windows, and it tells that the Government have decreed that the day after September 2nd should be September 14th. Eleven days are dropped; it is called – it is called the Gregorian Calendar, and I have forgotten about the rope."

The woman harshly laughed.

"Are you hearing me, Margaret?" he cried, putting up his arms to seize her, feeling some fresh terror.

"Gregorian here, Gregorian there!" she exclaimed. "Whose Calendar but the cursed Campbells', who have bonnily diddled me of my son! Our times are in God's hands, you said; you are witness now they are in the devil's!"

"But it may be I was right, and that this is our Father's miracle; John could not be – could not die but on the day appointed, and no such day, it seems, was on the Calendar. But I dared not ask, I dared not ask; I was dumfounded and ran to you, and here I am even without the rope."

Again the woman harshly laughed.

"You need not fash about the rope, goodman," said she; "at your very hand is plenty for your purpose, for there my son is, young John Clerk, and he hangs upon the tree."

The woman would not put a hand upon the body. Without her aid her husband lowered the burden from the gibbet, laid it in the cart and covered it with his plaid; and when a girth for the horse had been improvised from a part of the shameful halter, the two of them turned for home, walking side by side through the dawn that now was coming, slow and ashen, to the east.

The man was dumb, and walked without volition, wrestling with satanic doubts of a Holy Purpose that had robbed him of his son with such unnecessary and ghastly mockery; the woman cuddled her cold secret in her bosom, stared glassily at the coming day, and for a time let fury and despair whirl through her brain like poison vapours.

"I will never rest," she cried at last, "till Lochgair has paid the penalty for this trick upon us. My laddie's death is at his door!"

Her man said nothing, leading the horse.

"At his door!" she cried more vehemently. "Are you hearing me? He has slain my son in this shameful way as surely as if he had tied the rope himself."

Her husband made no answer; he found in her words but the thought of one for the time demented, and he walked appalled at the chaos into which the precious edifice of his faith had tumbled. Rudely she plucked his arm and screamed in his ear –

"What will you do to Campbell?"

"To Campbell?" he repeated vaguely. "God forgive him his false hopes and negligence, but it was not he who condemned our son."

"But for him," said the woman, "my son would have died like a gentleman, and not like a common thief."

"I do not understand," said her husband blankly.

"No, you never understand," she sneered, "that was ever your failing. Do you think that if I had not the promise of Lochgair, I should let my laddie die upon the gallows? The first of his race! the first of his race! I had brought with me his pistol that he might save himself the scandal of the doomster's hand," and she took the weapon from her bosom.

Her husband looked at it, grasped at once the Spartan spirit of her scheme, and swithered between chagrin that it had been foiled, and shame that the sin of self-slaughter should for a moment seem desirable.

"Oh, Margaret!" he cried, "you terrify me. Throw that dreadful weapon in the sea," and he made to take it from her, but she restored it to her plaid.

"No, no," she cried, "there may be use for it – "

"Use for it!" he repeated, and she poured into his ear the torrent of her hatred of Lochgair. "He could have won my laddie off," she said; "we had his own assurance. And if we had not put our trust in him, we would have gone to others – Asknish or Stonefield, or the Duke himself – the Duke would have had some pity on a mother."

"Lochgair may have sore deceived us," said her husband, "yet he was but an instrument; our laddie's doom was a thing appointed from the start of Time."

"Then from the start of Time you were doomed to slay Lochgair."

"What! I?" quo' he.

"One or other of us. We are, it seems by your religion, all in the hands of fate and cannot help ourselves. Stand up like a man to this filthy Campbell, and give him the bullet that was meant for a better man."

"You are mad, goodwife," said her husband; "I would shed no man's blood."

"I speak not of men," said she, "but of that false fiend Lochgair who has kept us on the rack, and robbed Time itself of a fortnight to make his clan diversion. Oh, man! man! are you a coward? Challenge him to the moor; remember that at the worst my son who lies in the cart there could have died in decency and not at the doomster's hand if Lochgair had not misled us – "

"Woman!" cried her husband, "get behind me!" and took refuge in a gust of mumbled prayer.

They were now upon the Kenmore shore where the sea came deep against the rocks; no living soul had met them on their passage down the coast with their disgraceful burden, and alarmed at the prospect of encounter with any curious wayfarer, they drew the cart behind a thicket, to let an approaching horseman pass without his observation. Far off they heard the clatter of his horse's hoofs, and while yet he was a good way distant the questing eye of the woman saw he wore a beaver hat, and a familiar coat with silver buttons!

"Look! look!" she cried, "here comes the very man, delivered to our hands."

"I will not touch him! I will not touch him!" said her husband, cowering behind the bushes.

"Then will I!" said she, and drew the pistol from her breast, and her husband wrestled with her for the weapon.

Lochgair in a furious haste came galloping, his vision engaged on the road before him, and would have swept on his way unnoticing the cart, its burden, or attendants, but for the altercation in the thicket. He checked his horse, turned round on the saddle, and peered among the branches, where the husband, breathing hard, had got possession of the weapon.

"He has slain my son, but I will spare him," said the husband, and the woman put her mouth against his ear.

"No son of yours," she whispered, "that is the curse of it! – but his own!"

"My God!" cried her husband, and fired at the horseman's breast. He fell like a sack of oats on the roadway, and his horse flew off among the brackens.

For a while the world seemed in a swound. In a swound the waves lapped up against the rocks; in a swound the leafage moved; in a swound the sea-birds cried, and the man and woman, desperate, sought to hide the evidence of their crime. They turned the dead man over on his back, emptied his pouches, filled his clothes with stones, then threw him, with the pistol, in the sea.

"Home! home!" the wife commanded, placing the dead man's papers in her plaid, and she walked, without remorse, by the side of her whimpering man, to Pennymore. She stirred the embers of the fire, and one by one destroyed the dead man's documents, until the very last, and that she glanced at horror-stricken, for it was her son's reprieve!

With a scream she rushed outside and turned her husband's plaid from the face of the dead man in the cart – and it was not young John Clerk!

A Return to Nature

I

THIS Highland country is so peaceful and content, its folk are so staid in welldoing, property is so safe, and the human passions – at least the more savage of them – are kept so strictly in control, that most of us forget how lately we rose from the rude condition of nature. It is really but a brief span of years that separates us from our fathers who slept with an ear to the heather, hunted in the forests for their very lives, fought in stupid causes as heartily as we go football-playing, or forayed over narrow borders into parts of the country distinguished from their own but by a difference in the colour of the tartan. Who thinks of the ancient cateran fire smouldering under a frock-coat, or would imagine that the cry of "Cruachan!" in the ears of a quiet and prosperous sheep-farmer at a country fair will sometimes splash deep in the wells of his being, and stir up the red ghosts of war and vengeance that have not walked for generations? I have seen that marvel often, though always with new astonishment. I can amuse myself sometimes by saying one word of great meaning to the members of a family that has not broken the law since the year 1745, and see, in a moment, bitterness where before was indifference, anger in the gentlest girls, and in their brothers a hate almost as unreasoning and hot as that of Cain. A flash – just one flash of the spirit that we do not control, but with no consent of the flesh – and then they will laugh at their own folly.

It was some such flame of the ancient elemental passions, doubtless, that accounted for the transgression of Macaulay, the factor of the Captain of Kilree – an out-break of the Islands that I think has had no parallel in the annals of Scotland for more than a hundred years. I did not know Macaulay in his prime. When I was a boy he was an ancient, bent, and spiritless man, with a singularly devout reputation, and a grim, humorsome Lowland wife; but everybody round the countryside knew his story, and we boys used to look at him from afar off, amazed, admiring, and half-incredulous, like children who have heard tales of giants who could stride from hill to hill, and have at last been taken to see one in a show. In his shabby green business suit of broadcloth and beaver hat, or leaning on his cane at the church gate, with snuff strewn down his waistcoat, there was nothing at all about his personality to suggest the terrific and romantic. Maybe, as our elders used to say, the nose did hint at the eagle, the flaring nostril say something of the morning sniffed suspiciously among alders where the skulker hid, a certain twitch of the bushy eyebrows express a fearful soul that one time stood alone on hill-tops and saw the whole visible world its enemy; but to our vision, at least, the man was "done," as we say, and by his look might have been a prosperous weaver in the decline of years.

Yet he had an experience, the narration of which by our elders gave him the glory of Rob Roy to our imaginations. He had, in a sublime hour of his life, burst the bonds that make some of us fret in the urging weather of spring, that most of us chafe at in childhood, when the old savage wakes and cries, but grow at last to tolerate and even cherish; and he had taken the world for his pillow – as the Gaelic phrase goes – and short of the vital blood of man had dipped in the early sins.

II

Alexander Macaulay was his name; in the common conversation of the people he was known as Alasdair Dhu, or Black Alick, for till he was nearly seventy his hair was like the bramble-berry. Of his forebears in the island everybody knew; they had owned Kincreggan for at least five hundred years, until, in his grandfather's time, they were proscribed and rendered fugitive, made Children of the Mist, nameless vagabonds frequenting desolate straths, making uneasy beds on hunted moors, their home reft from them more by the quirk of the law than by valour, and the walls of it grown with nettle and fern on the verge of the forest of Kilree. Himself he had been brought up far apart from the scenes of his cateran family, in a decent humdrum fashion in the Low Country, where he had studied the law, and whence he had come to his native isle a writer. Silent, they said of him – silent and dour, except in congenial company, when his laugh was as ready as any one's, and his sense of a joke singularly shrewd. Just a plain, douce, decent lawyer body, given pedantically to the quotation of Latin maxims affecting his profession; married, as I have said, to a Lowland wife; his business comfortable, bringing him much about the Islands in boats and gigs. He was "doer" – which is to say, man of business, or agent – for several of the most notable families in the shire in his later years; but at the time I speak of he was factor for Kilree alone.

When I have added that he was forty years of age when he had his odd relapse, could sing a fine bass to the Psalmody on a Sabbath, was great for books, and thought no hour of the day so happy as when he could get into his slippers and his feet on the fender, and drink a dish of tea – a beverage for which he had a passion many men have for wine – I have summed up all that was apparent to his neighbours in the character of Alexander

Macaulay. And yet they left out a great part of the real Macaulay in their estimate of the factor of Kilree.

It happened on a dirty wet day in the month of May that Kilree the Captain himself was on the island, and came to Macaulay's office to consult regarding some improvements – as he esteemed them – that he had for long contemplated on the inland side of his estate. He was in the Army, a good and gallant soul, young and sentimental, with what is even now common enough in the Highlands and Islands, a great regard for old romantics.

"And I start at once to put the fence from Cairn Dearg to Carsaig," said he by-and-by, carelessly walking up and down Macaulay's room, and looking through the window at the sea-birds flying noisily along the shore.

The lawyer gave a little start in his arm-chair, and upset a bottle of red ink. It was dripping from the desk to his knees, and he hurriedly swept his hand across the stream of it, then dashed the flood with sand. "To Carsaig, did you say?" he asked, taking up his penknife in his reddened hand and nervously starting to shape a quill.

"Yes," said the Captain, suspecting nothing. "Time's slipping past, and I'm determined to put off no longer carrying out my father's old notion of having the fence as far as the two rivers."

"And what about Kincreggan?" asked the lawyer, suddenly grown the colour of clay, but sitting still at his desk, his eyes on his reddened hand, some strange freak of the fancy, as he used to say in after years, filling his head with the salt scent of blood. Kincreggan, his people's home before they were broken, and tenants of the mist alone, was in a little glen of Carsaig. In his mind in a moment he saw it perched above its waters, empty and cold and grey, with only memory under its rotting rafters.

"Oh, Kincreggan! Damn Kincreggan!" said the Captain, quite forgetting that ever a Macaulay was bred there. "Kincreggan comes down, of course; I'm going to put a shepherd's cottage there."

"What! you will pull down Kincreggan House," cried the lawyer, jumping to his feet so suddenly that his chair upset behind him. "Kincreggan!" he repeated, with a kind of whimper; and the Captain turned sharply round at the strangeness of the cry, and saw another man than his customary factor – a fellow all thong in every sinew of his neck and face, his hair tossed on his temples, his arms strained back, and a bloody hand clenched, his whole body stiff as if he were about to spring. And his eyes were wells of fire.

"Good God! what cat-a-mountain have I here in Alasdair Macaulay?" thought the Captain, startled, and then remembered whose Kincreggan had been.

"Kincreggan!" said the lawyer again, and followed with a phrase of the Gaelic language that he had never been known to speak since he left the island, a child, for Edinburgh.

"Upon my word," said the Captain, "but I clean forgot the old connection! How was I to know my factor had the least objection? Come, come, Mr Macaulay, we cannot permit a foolish old sentiment about a ruin of stones to stand in the way of honest improvement. It is not as if Kincreggan was a castle or a cathedral. I have my own repugnances about spoiling old landmarks, but Kincreggan – Come, come, Mr Macaulay, what scruple need there be about a place like yon! Beyond yourself there is not a single soul of the old breed left, and you never saw a fire in it – no, nor your father before you!"

No miracle imaginable could have surprised him more than this – that a plain man of the law in broadcloth in a carpeted office, with a pile of black deed-boxes behind him, and the statutes of the land calf-bound on a shelf at his elbow, a pen in his hand, and a fob-chain dangling below his waistcoat, could have so remarkable a sentiment about an old ruin as these dramatics of his seemed to suggest.

"Pooh! Mr Macaulay," said he, "ye need not make any fracas about it now, for Mackay has his orders, and starts at Kincreggan immediately; the roof will be off in a day or two. And as for these silly clan sentiments, I have lost money by them ere this: I will let them influence me no more; I do not value them that, Mr Macaulay!" And so saying, he cracked his fingers in his factor's face.

Alasdair Dhu felt his blood boil in his head till his skull seemed like to burst; the stain on his hand enlarged to a crimson cloud that filled the chamber, as he used in later years to say himself, and a strange roaring came into his ears. Suddenly he gave the cry of his clan, ran up against Kilree, and with the penknife stabbed him in the bosom.

Without a pause so little as to look at the victim of his frenzy, he passed quickly into his house, whereof his writing chamber was a part. His wife sat sewing. He looked at her with an ecstasy in his eyes: "I'm sick-tired of this," cried he; "my grief! but I have been wasting time." And so saying, he turned on his heel and ran out to the garden behind the house. Knowing nothing of the Captain's state, she ran out after her husband, and saw him leap the wall like a young roe. His clerk, a lad Macdonald, was out in the garden for peats for the office fire. "Look at your master!" she cried, and together they watched the lawyer throw off his coat as he ran, and disappear at last in the fir planting on the other side of the road, whence it rose on the face of the hill.

"What a caper!" she exclaimed. "Tut! tut! – he's daft – clean daft! I always thought there was a lot of his grandfather, Ranald, in him. And such a day! He'll get wet to the skin."

III

Kincreggan is in a cleft of the mountain where the River Glas is joined by the Water of Maam, its situation chosen with cunning for that purpose it used so well to serve. For weeks after the lawyer had ludicrously cast off his coat on the highway and disposed of his trews in the planting behind his office, and was seen making for Kilree forest wrapped ingeniously in a web of tartan filched from a weaver's waulking-wicker, Kincreggan, for all the Isles, at least, was the most interesting place in the world. People quitted work, put on their Sabbath clothes, and came a long day's journey to see it, not approaching it by the narrow pass that led to its front walls, but laboriously climbing the hills from whose tops they could in safety get a view of the old place where there had so suddenly flared up fires dead two hundred years.

What they saw – all they could see – was a grey whinstone tower built extraordinarily with its back against Cnoc Dearg, a red precipice hundreds of feet high, a gable and front to the very edge of the rock that hung over a deep dark pool made by the falls at the fork of the rivers, its main gable opening on the cattle-fold and the pass that gave the only entrance to Kincreggan. They saw a place as ill to storm as though it crowned a mountain, a place devised strictly for hours of war – but still a beautiful place, wherein a person of fancy might be content to dwell for ever as in a petty kingdom, the fish of the pool his, the birds that clucked or sang in the alder thickets round the fold at the mountain foot, the deer that came down for the sun of the afternoon, the cattle that lowed in the pen.

And Alasdair Dhu had the cattle! The people could see them plainly from the hill, and in certain puffs of the spring wind hear their *geumnaich* – the sad complaint that Highland kyloes make on strange pastures, remembering the sweeter taste of the grass of home. The cattle were Kilree's. They had gone from his hill at night as by magic, and in the morning they were in Kincreggan fold, where stolen herds were harboured before the old Macaulays went into the mist, and where there had not been a hoof in four generations. With the cattle, furthermore, went missing a number of muskets from the armoury of Kilree. Macaulay the lawyer was back at his forefathers' business!

The first thing a man to-day would do in the like circumstances would be to call for the police; but even to-day, in the Islands, the police are rare and remote from Kilree, and at that time it was as ill to reach them as to reach St Kilda, even had there been no popular conviction that the civil law alone is all that a Highland gentleman can with propriety call into action. So Kilree for a while did nothing but nurse his wound, and Macaulay lurked in his fastness alone, no one – by the Captain's orders – lifting a hand against him. But the stabbing of his master and the lifting of his bestial were only the start of his escapade, which became the more astonishing after his clerk, the lad Macdonald, out of Moidart, was sent to him on a curious mission.

Macdonald was a fellow without fear, and it must be added, without brains either, otherwise he might never have done a thing that made all the Isles laugh at him when they heard later what he had carried, and another thing that bears out my premiss that the primitive man is immediately below a good many well-laundered modern shirts.

"I think I could bring that madman of mine to his senses," Macaulay's wife said to the clerk one day.

"The sooner the better, then," said Macdonald, "for there's much to do before the rent collection." He spoke as if his master were only out upon a drinking-bout.

"If I just had him here for ten minutes!" said Mrs Macaulay.

"You might – you might venture to go to Kincreggan and see him," suggested the clerk.

"I have more regard for my life," said the woman. "I'm ower much of the Lowlander to trust myself in a den with a mad Highlander – even if he's my own man. Forbye" (here she smiled), "forbye, I've tried it already. I have been twice at Kincreggan in the early morning, and he kept me fifty yards off the walls with his gun. But I would not care to have that mentioned in the place; it's perhaps as little to my credit as to his own. Oh, if I had him under this roof again for ten minutes, or could get a certain thing delivered in his hands –" She broke off, and looked into Macdonald's face quickly as with an inspiration.

"What is it?" asked the clerk.

"A little packet," she replied; "just a small packet you could carry in your hand."

"*Buidseachas?* – I mean witchcraft?" said Macdonald, who had brought a good many superstitions from Moidart.

"Well, well – in a way, a sort of witchcraft," she admitted, with a smile. "It is part of a charm that wiles men from their wild ways."

"I don't know but what I might risk taking it to him, then," said Macdonald, and so it happened that that very evening he found himself challenged fifty yards from the wall of Kincreggan, with a pair of slippers wrapped carefully in paper in his hands – nothing more.

"What have you there, Macdonald?" cried the master, girning over the neck of a musket at his clerk, who shook on the edge of the river at the narrowest part of the pass.

"I do not know," was the lad's answer, for indeed his knowledge of what he carried was due to his own curiosity and not to any information he had got from the lady who sent him. "I do not know; I was sent with it by your wife, Mr Macaulay."

"Kincreggan, you mean," corrected the factor, plainly determined on the old territorial honours.

"Kincreggan."

"Drop it into the pool, then," commanded the madman, snuggling closer to his weapon, and Macdonald did as he was told.

"Now come in and I will speak to you," said Macaulay, and so the clerk got into Kincreggan, and however his master coaxed or cozened him, he stayed there.

For some days after the cracking of guns was heard echoing for miles round the hollow of Kincreggan. That sent the island mad with an itching curiosity. On all the roads men and women travelled, and up the face of Ben Buidhe, to lie on the myrtle and look at Alasdair Dhu and his clerk shooting and fishing as in the fine free ancient days. It was no secret that many admired the outlaw; his state of nature seemed so enviable compared with their own poor prosaic lives as fishers or shepherds, that he might have had recruits if he had been more accessible. The people were vexed for the Captain, it is true, but not so vexed that they could not admire the cleverness of the man who, bred in towns and brought up to the pen, had lifted the laird's cattle as neatly as if he had tramped a lifetime through night and mist with his forebears. They got a new light upon society and its rights and wrongs, though they might not have the philosophy to explain it clearly; they seemed to see that might was right at any time; they searched themselves in vain to see wherein Macaulay and his clerk, possessing themselves of Macaulay's ancient home and of things not made with hands, but nature's gifts, were any worse than the long line of Kilree's family that, ending in the Captain himself, had used cunning and contrivance to get and keep these things. It was said that a kind of fever went through the men when they saw the example of Macaulay, that they abandoned their common tasks awhile, and might, but for mothers and wives, have gone wholly wrong.

The Captain was no sooner out of his doctor's hands than he sent a corps of his workmen to expel the outlaws and pull down Kincreggan House.

"By heavens!" he said, "I'm hardly angry at the fellow for his mischievousness; it takes so uncommon a form. He might have robbed me all these years decently like a man of business in quite another fashion far less interesting. It's madness, of course, but it's in a lot of blood that runs very sluggishly in these parts nowadays. I sometimes have had a touch of it myself, so I'll give the rogue law."

Up to Kincreggan, then, went his men with picks, and the first of them had only got round the bend of the pass when a bullet flew over his head and another close behind it. The lawyer and his clerk were determined to hold Kincreggan as Ranald More Macaulay had held it against the Captain's grandfather!

Next the Captain himself went up, and reached as far as the wall of the fold where his own cattle were imprisoned. A cry stopped him at the wall, and he looked up to see the pieces of Macaulay and the lad directed at his breast.

"A parley, Kincreggan!" he cried, slyly giving his late factor the honour.

The lawyer was hard to recognise, so oddly had he changed from the shaven and well-put-on man of business who had plied an industrious quill but lately at a desk. A beard blackened his face; the pilfered web of tartan was belted round his loins into a kilt, with the end of it dragged round his shoulder for a plaid in the fashion of the age of Mar; a blue bonnet was scrugged down upon his brow, and on his feet, that used to enjoy the slippers of his own fireside, were *cuarains* – roughly-made moccasins of ox-hide with the hair still on them. It was, to the eye and imagination of the Captain, as if time and change had someway overlooked the shelter of Kincreggan in its mountain cleft, and there had remained in it, unknown and unsuspected, some eddying backwater of the wild old days. In faith, Macaulay in such an ancient polity had been a chief of chiefs; he had it in his aspect and his mien. He stood against the crenels of a bastion, his whole figure revealed, an elbow on the stones and the musket balanced in his hands, a kind of lazy elegance in his attitude, ease and independence, health and pride. He looked at his old client as an eagle might look at a lamb, swithering whether he should swoop or stay still. The only thing to mar the dignity of the picture was the presence of his clerk in an angle of the wall besides him – still the 'prentice lawyer, doubtless even to the ink on the very finger that hung on the trigger of the weapon with which he covered the Captain.

"I will be giving you three minutes, Kilree," said Macaulay, "to get the length of the boulder yonder on your way back. If I see so much as your heel after that I will shoot at it, and you will not escape with your life a second time."

"That is very fine, and I'll not deny it is picturesque," said the Captain, "but it's a little out of date and a cursed folly. More than that, it's robbery, to say nothing about the – the accident with the knife, and nowadays there's admitted to be no grace about a robbery even committed in a kilt. It might be all very well for your grandfather and my own to fight like this over these walls, but – "

"How did Kincreggan come into the hands of your family?" interrupted the lawyer.

"You have me there," admitted the Captain, with a little awkward laugh. "You have me there, and I'm not a lawyer to obscure the facts. Our folk fought yours for it, and having got it – "

"Well, the fighting was not finished," said the outlaw; "I have begun it again, and Kincreggan is Macaulay's. Go back, Kilree, go back; and if you come again, bring a coffin under your arm."

The Captain went, and it was the last he was to see of his factor till that stormy Lammas day when the outlaw came home.

Macaulay roved the moors and forest while his clerk kept ward in their fortress. Stags fell to his gun, the best linns gave him fish. At the market in Marinish, over the ford on the other island, where the Captain's clan was unpopular, Macaulay one day appeared at a cattle tryst and sold beasts the buyers did not inquire too closely about, and he replaced them in his fold with others lifted boldly from Kilree's home farm on his way back from the market. Night and day he was watched for, but night or day either he or Macdonald was awake and waiting; and more than once he was at the other end of the parish on some exploit while Kilree's men kept an eye on the pass.

He became the glory of his own island, and a toast at fairs in all the Islands. "Alasdair Dhu" was the name on every lip; his wife shared his popularity, and people sent her gifts of sheep and fowl from as far as the mainland. And all she would say was, "What a silly thing! An island of men against one man in a dream! If I had just had him here!"

IV

The Captain, who had been with his corps in the Lowlands, came home, thought hard, and made a plan. "If my factor is so fond of nature, I must fight him with that same," he said, and for two weeks before Lammas he had every man in his service building a dam below the pass of Kincreggan. It was so clever a way of getting the better of Alasdair Dhu that the men who admired him most now turned most readily to spoil him. They cut down big firs on either side of the pass, so that the trees fell over and jammed between the cliffs. When the pile was high enough they backed it up with brushwood and turf till it looked like a lofty wall.

"I'm thinking that will do now," said the Captain when it was done. "Let us have the first of the floods of Lammas, and you will see a rat come squealing from his hole."

When the dam was finished it was dry weather, the river at the pass a trickle; but the Captain's own luck was with him, for the very next day a storm burst on the Islands. He went to the top of Ben Buidhe, and joined the folk there who were looking down on Kincreggan. They saw a spectacle! The river, pit-black in its linns and cream-white in its falls, gulped down the narrow gorge as if all the waters of the world were hasting there; the cliff above the keep was streaming, the path to the house was flooded, the cattle were belly-deep in the fold, and bellowed mournfully. Every minute saw the water perceptibly rise till it lay like a loch deep about Kincreggan House. By the time the gloaming came on the glen the water washed the lintels of the lower storey.

"It's a dour rat, by my troth!" said the Captain. "I thought we would have heard squealing by this time."

He shook the rain from his plaid, and set off for home. Some say he was heedless of Macaulay's fate; others more plausibly argue that he knew very well Macaulay had friends on the hillside who would rescue him when the need arose.

However it was Macaulay got out of his trap, he got out by himself, with his clerk behind him. The lad ran over the island, took a boat to Arisaig, and never came back again; the factor reached the door of his home at dark – an amazing figure in drenched and savage garments, with a dirk lying flat against the brawn of his bare arm. He burst upon his wife like a calamity, but she never blenched. The kettle hung upon its chain; with a thrust of her foot she swung it over the fire, and rose to her feet to put a hand on the shoulder of her soaking lord.

"Oh, Alick! come in, come in!" she said, and so mighty he looked and strange in the room that had known the decent lawyer, it seemed to her as if he filled it. The river ran from his garments, and when he moved, the hides on his feet sucked upon the flooring.

"They tell me at Kilree the Captain is here," he said, looking uplifted about him, keeping the blade of his weapon out of her sight.

"He is just come," she answered, "and is in front there, keeping your place for you."

A devilish satisfaction betrayed itself in Macaulay's face. "I have tasted life," he said, stretching out his arms, and gloating, as it seemed, upon himself. "I have tasted life, and I would not change with kings! All the clan cries in me, and I am proud, proud! But there is one thing wanting: I will make sure of him this time," and saying that, he flourished the dirk and made for the door that led to his writing chamber.

His wife gave a cry, and put herself before him. "Oh, Alick!" she said, as calm as she could be, "you are very wet; at least you will first of all put on dry hose and take a dish of tea," pushing him gently at the same time towards his accustomed chair. He fondled his weapon, and sat in the humour of one who is willing to put off a pleasure that it may be greater by delay. She plucked the *cuarains* from his feet and put on him hose and slippers, all in a nervous haste, and the slippers were no sooner on his feet than he shook himself, looked with disgust on his drenched tartan, and threw the dirk away.

"My God!" said he; "what cantrip is this?"

"You will have a dish of tea," said the wife, hurriedly preparing it; and he wriggled his toes in the slippers and sat closer to the fire, cherishing its warmth with that accustomed manner he forgot the day he went astray. Again and again he looked at himself, and, sipping the tea, "What a folly! What a folly!" he would utter. "What put such mischief in my brain? And we were over head and ears with business at the office! I must work night and day if I am to be ready for the rents. Young Macdonald, too! Tut, tut! the thing was fair ridiculous! I'm black affronted. Flora, woman, haste ye and get my breeks!"

The discarded broadcloth was put out; he sheared and shaved himself before the glass till the wild man of the mountain was gone, and emerged the lawyer, then walked into his writing chamber.

"Good evening, Captain," he said briskly to his client, just as if he had been out for an airing. "This has been a stupid business – a remarkably stupid business. I must crave your pardon. At such an inconvenient time, too! But I hope to make it up some way."

The Captain could scarcely trust his senses. He had risen to defend himself against the savage, and here was his sober man of business back!

"Well, it has been what might be called a fairly busy summer with us, Mr Macaulay," said the Captain, at his wits' end how to meet so curious a penitent. "And I have still got a twinge of your penknife in my breast now and then."

The factor's face reddened. "I declare, I'm affronted," said he. "With a penknife! Tut, tut! – a villainously silly weapon, Captain; and still it might have been a serious enough thing for you. I'm beat to understand it; some lesion of the brain, as the medical jurisprudists say; I would never harm a cat, except *durante furore* – if – if I deliberated on it. I have little doubt I'm the talk of the country – most annoying, most annoying! I should not wonder if the profession made it the occasion of a complaint against me; and if it come to that, sir, I hope I may look for your support?"

He took up his penknife again – it still lay on his desk – and the Captain stood back from him abruptly, but he need not have done so, for the lawyer was only going to sharp his pen, as benign and proper a man as ever charged a fee. His client did not know whether to laugh or storm. He felt like to laugh at the ludicrousness of the way Macaulay had returned to his senses; he felt anger with the unaccountable spirit which made the offender more perturbed about the figure he must henceforth cut in public than that he should for a summer have played the part of robber, and wellnigh been a murderer too. But the good humour of Kilree prevailed, and he laughed – a demonstration that but visibly increased Macaulay's chagrin.

"It is no laughing affair, I assure you – at least for me," said he. "Here I am six months behind with my work, and I doubt not all my correspondents furious."

"Mrs Macaulay and I between us have made shift to deal with the correspondence in your – in your holiday," said the laird. "The most serious thing, I'm thinking, is a drove of cattle sold by Alasdair Dhu at Marinish tryst; I'm too poor a man to afford the loss of them."

"You will not lose a penny," said Macaulay. "I got the best of prices for them, and have the money now. It was an irregularity."

"So one might call it," agreed the Captain.

"It was an irregularity, a sudden craze. If I had been a man who drank –"

"You would probably have drowned the flame of folly long before now," said the Captain, who sometimes took a dram.

"A flame, exactly! Just a flame; no word better describes it. When you spoke of taking down that rotten den, I was for the time possessed. I can honestly tell you that a score of thoughts came sweeping through me that I never harboured for a second in my life before."

"Nor had intruded on you before, eh, Macaulay?" said the Captain.

"That – that is neither here nor there; if every man confessed the thoughts his better nature rejected we were all condemned for the gallows sooner or later."

"I must say I was looking for a little more contrition, Mr Macaulay," said the Captain. "You'll allow the escapade was a little unusual, and not without some inconvenience to myself? You seem to take it in so odd a spirit that I cannot be sure against a recurrence. I may tell you that I'm determined to have Kincreggan down – I can be as dour as yourself, you see – and though I might be prepared to fight the point of its ownership once in the old fashion, I cannot guarantee that I should be ready for that a second time."

"Not a word!" said Macaulay hastily. "My position was ridiculous in law and equity. *Ne dominia rerum sint incerta neve lites sint perpetuæ* – even if your folk had held the place for only forty years instead of two hundred, your claim would be unassailable, as I'm prepared to contest in any court in the land. Kincreggan, Captain – pooh! I esteem the place so little that upon my word I would not grudge to put powder to it myself. And, if you will permit me, I'll take my desk again."

Kilree rose from the lawyer's seat with a chuckle, and Macaulay, indicating another, sank into his old chair with a sigh of satisfaction.

"I would like to ask you one thing," said the Captain. "How did it feel?"

The lawyer flushed over his clean-shaven face and stared straight in front of him out of the window at the sea-shore with the wild gulls flying free.

"I hope it is the last time so shameful an affair will call for reference," he said; "but I'll tell you this, it was – it was an ecstasy! I would not have lost the experience for ten thousand pounds."

"Ho! ho!" said the Captain.

"Nor have it again for twice ten thousand," concluded the lawyer.

"And do you know this?" said the Captain, taking a grip of his arm and speaking softly into his ear. "Do you know this? By heavens, I envy you! What broke the spell?"

"I know, but I'm not going to tell you," said the lawyer shamefacedly.

"Come, come! It is hardly worth while swallowing the rump and retching at the tail."

"Between ourselves, then," replied Macaulay, "it was my slippers. That and an indifferent dish of tea. If my wife had not got me into my slippers, neither you nor I would be sitting so jocular here. The freedom of the mountains is not to be compared with a pair of dry hose and content beside the fire."

At that the Captain grimaced. "Tut!" said he. "I wish I had not asked you. I expected a miracle, and you give me only an epitome of civilisation."

The Brooch

WANLOCK of Manor looked with a puckered face at the tiny jewel flaming in the hollow of his hand, and, for the hour forswearing piety, cursed the lamented Lady Grace, his sister, *haut en bas*, with all the fury of his bitter disappointment. The harridan had her revenge! Last night he dreamt her envoys by their wailings made the forest hideous; already amongst the Shadows of the monstrous other world she must be chuckling (if the Shades have laughter) through her toothless gums at the chagrin of her brother, for the first of the seven shocks of evil fortune had that moment staggered him, and he was smitten to the vitals in his purse and pride.

The brooch, so wretchedly inadequate as consolation for the legacy he had long anticipated, had seemed last night as he peered at it with dubious eyes a bauble wholly innocent, and he laughed at its sinister reputation, which in a last vagary of her spiteful humour she had been at pains to apprise him of in a posthumous private letter. "Seven shocks of dire disaster, and the last the worst," he had read in the crabbed writing of the woman who, even in prosperity, could never pardon him his luckless speculation with the money that was meant to be her dowry; he had sneered at her pagan folly, but now the premonstration bore a different aspect; he was stunned with the news that his law-plea with Paul Mellish of The Peel was lost, and that the bare expenses of that long-protracted fight should cost him all that was left of his beggared fortunes. But that was not the worst of it, for Mellish, as in pity of a helpless foe, had waived his admitted claim to the swampy field which was the object of their litigation. The first blow, surely, with a vengeance!

For a moment Wanlock, now assured of some uncanny essence in the jewel, thought to defend himself by its immediate destruction, and then he had a craftier inspiration. He strode across the room, threw up the window-sash, and bellowed upon Stephen, his idle son, the spoiled monopolist of what love he had to spare.

"You see this brooch?" he said when the lad, with a grey dog at his heels, came in with a rakish swagger from his interrupted dalliance with the last maid (so to call her) left of Wanlock's retinue.

They looked at it together as it lay in the father's hand – a garnet, cut *en cabochon*, smoothly rounded like a blob of claret by the lapidary, clasped by thin gold claws; and the dog, with eyes askance, stood near them, wrapt in cogitations of a different world. Their heads went down upon the gem: they stared in silence, strangely influenced by its eye-like shape and sullen glow, that seemed to come less from the polished surface than from a cynic spirit inward, animate. It had the look of age: had glowed on the breasts of high-scarfed dandies, pinned the screens on girlish bosoms flat now in the dust, known the dear privacies of love and passion, lurked in the dusk of treasuries, kept itself unspotted, indifferent, unchanged through the flux of human generations. Lord! that men's lives should be so short and the objects of their fashioning so permanent!

"It may be braw, but it's no' very bonny," at the last quo' Stephen Wanlock.

"I want ye," said his father, "to take it now with – with my assurance of regard and – and gratitude to Mellish of The Peel. He has a craze for such gewgaws, with no small part of his money, they tell me, sunk in their collection. You can say it has the reputation of a charm."

Young Wanlock posted off on this pleasant mission, with a chuck below the chin for the maid in passing; and his father, walking in the afternoon between the dishevelled shrubberies of his neglected policies, felt at times amid the anguish of his situation a soothing sense of other ills averted and transferred to one whom now he hated worse than ever.

It seemed next day as if the evil genius dwelling in the jewel wrought its purpose with appalling expedition. Something is in the air of our haunted North whose beaked sea promontories cleave the wind and foam, that carries the hint of things impending to all who have boding fears or hateful speculations, and Wanlock knew some blow had fallen on his enemy while yet there were no human tidings. The pyots chattered garrulous as women on the walls; the rooks that flew across the grey storm-bitten country were in clanging bands, possessed of rumours which they shared at first with the careering clouds alone, for men are the last of all created things to learn of their own disasters.

He went eagerly out and came on other harbingers. A horseman galloped down the glen – "The Peel! The Peel!" he cried, as he thundered past with his head across his shoulder – "They have broken The Peel!" A running gypsy with a mountain of shining cans a-clatter on his back skulked into the wood as Wanlock came upon him, and harried forth by the dog, stood on the highway wildly protesting innocence.

"Who blamed ye?" queried Wanlock. "What has happened?"

"I declare to my God I know nothing of it!" cried the man in an excess of apprehension, "but The Peel, they say, was broken into through the night."

"Ha! say ye so!" said Wanlock, kindling. "The wicked flee when no man pursueth: ye run gey fast, I think, for innocence," and he fixed a piercing gaze upon the wretch, who drew his hand across his throat and held it up to heaven.

"But it is none of my affair – begone!" said Wanlock, and the gypsy clattered on his way.

Wanlock leaned upon his cane, with the grey dog at his heels, and let the exultation of the tidings well through all his being. The woods were sombre round about him: silent and sad, bereft of voices, for it was the summer's end, and birds were grieving their departed children. And yet not wholly still, the forest, for in its dark recesses something unexpressive moved and muttered. His joy ebbed out, his new mistrusts beset him; with a wave of the hand he sent the dog among the undergrowth, and when it disappeared, there rose among the tangle of the wood an eerie call, indefinite, despondent, like a dirge. Had the land itself a voice and memory of a golden age of sunshine and eternal Spring, thus might it be lamenting. But still – but still 'twas not a voice of nature, rather to the ear of Wanlock like the utterance of a creature lost in some strange country looking for home and love. So call the fallen angels in the interspace, remembering joys evanished.

A hand fell on the listener's shoulder: he flinched and turned to look in the face of his daughter Mirren.

"Have you heard the news?" she asked him, breathing deeply, with a wan and troubled aspect.

He held up an arresting hand, and "Hush!" he said, "there is something curious in the wood... Did ye not hear it? Something curious in the wood... In the wood... Did ye not... did ye not hear it?" and his head sank down upon his shoulders; his eyes went questing through the columns of the trees.

Again the cry rose, farther in the distance, burdened with a sense of desolation.

"A bittern," said Mirren; "it can only be a bittern."

"Do ye think I have not thought of that?" asked Wanlock. "Have ye ever heard a bittern boom at this time of the year, and in the middle of the day?"

"I have heard it once or twice at night of late," said his daughter. "It can only be a bittern, or some other creature maybe wounded. Do you know that The Peel has been plundered? Last night the strong-room was broken into."

"And robbed of the Mellish jewels?" broke in Wanlock, with exultant intuition.

"Yes, and a great collection of antique gems entrusted to Mellish for the purpose of a monograph he was writing," said the daughter.

"A monograph?" asked Wanlock, still with eyes bent on the wood from which the dog returned indifferent.

"It is a book on gems he has been busy writing."

Wanlock sneered. "A book!" said he. "I'm thinking he'd be better at some other business. I find, myself, but the one Book needful; all the others are but vanity, and lead but to confusion. And he was pillaged, was he? Well, there's this, it might have been a man who could afford it less, for Mellish was the wealthiest in the shire."

"But now he is the poorest," said the girl with pity. "I'm told it means his utter ruin."

"There's the money of the Glasfurd girl to patch his broken fortune with; they're long enough engaged if the clash of the countryside be true," said Wanlock, and his daughter blenched, while the wailing cry rose up again beyond the fir-tops on the moorland edge.

Wanlock stood confused a moment, then seized her by the arm. "Would ye have me vexed for him?" said he. "Now I – with your permission – look upon it as a dispensation. If Mellish is ruined, Dreghorn is the richest man in the countryside and the better match for you –"

"Dreghorn!" cried the girl with scorn. "He danced at my mother's wedding – a cankered, friendless miser!"

"And now he'll dance at yours! There have been men more spendthrift, I'll admit, but you're not a Wanlock if in that respect ye could not teach him better. He was at me again for ye yesterday –"

Mirren put her fingers in her ears; she was used to these importunities; they had lately made her days and nights unhappy, and sent her fleeing like a wild thing to the hills, or roving with a rebel heart in all the solitary places of the valley. At any other hour this spirit would have made him furious; to-day he was elated at her news, and let her go.

His joy, however, was but transitory. Searching with a candle late that evening through his wine-cellar among dusty bins whose empty niches gloomily announced the ebbing tide of that red sea of pleasure, or its ficti- tious wave, that had swept so high on ancient jovial nights to the lips of many generations of the guests of Manor, a yellow glint as from a reptile's eye fastened upon him from a cobwebbed corner. He stared at it in horror and unbelief, closed in upon it with his guttering candle, warily, and found himself once more the owner of the brooch!

In the chill of the vault he felt, for a moment, the convulsion of a mind confronted with some vast mysterious power whose breath was loathsome, deathly, redolent of dust and fraught with retribution, and fearing an actual presence, almost shrieked when the flame of his candle was extinguished in the draught of a slowly opening door. He stood all trembling, with the jewel in his hand: a mocking chuckle rose in the outer night: all the old eerie tales of childhood then were true! He heard approaching cautious footsteps; a light was struck; a taper flared, and he faced the ne'er-do-well, his son!

"At the wine again, Stephen?" he said with unspeakable sadness, for indeed the lad had been the apple of his eye, and he knew too well his failing.

"Not this time, father!" said the son, with some effrontery in spite of his perturbation. "There's damned little left between us: we're at the dregs of the old Bordeaux. I dropped – I dropped something last time I was here, I fancy, and I'm come to seek for it."

His father's cheek in the daytime would have ashened: in the taper light it merely shook and crinkled colourlessly like a scum. He held the brooch out in his hand, and asked, "Is that it, Stephen?" in the simple phrase of a man with his last illusion shattered, and the son confessed.

He had been shown to the strong-room when he carried the brooch to Mellish: the sight of its contents and all their possibilities of life and pleasure had fevered him with desire: he had returned in cover of night and plundered the treasure of The Peel.

"Oh Lord!" cried Wanlock, "must I now pay teind to hell? 'He that begetteth a fool doeth it to his own sorrow, and the father of a fool hath no joy.' And where, my rogue, have ye put your plunder?"

"That is the worst of it," said Stephen: "you have it all there in your hand! It lay apart from the rest, and I put it in my pocket."

"A liar, too!" wailed Wanlock.

"It is nothing but the truth," protested Stephen sullenly. "I was observed, whether by man or woman, beast or bogle, I cannot tell, but I heard the laugh at my elbow, and I ran. It pattered at my heels, and would have caught me if I had not dropped my burden in the old Peel well."

"And there let it lie and rot!" exclaimed his father. "But you – oh, Stephen! – you to be the robber! and bring on me the second blow!" and the wine-vault rang with the blame and lamentation of a shattered man.

The son was packed off on the morrow lest a worse thing should befall in a suspicion of his part in the fall of Mellish: his father paid the last penny of his available money for the journey to the south; the search for the spoiler passed into other parts of the country, and was speedily abandoned. When the hue and cry had ceased, old Wanlock, professing to have found the brooch on the roadside, sent it back to Mellish, and waited with a savage expectation for another demonstration of its power.

He had not long to wait. The very day on which the talisman was sent, the match of Mellish with the Glasfurd girl – as rich as she was proud, haughty, and ambitious – was broken off by one who could not bring herself to marry a beggared man, and the tale, by gossip amplified and rendered almost laughable, went round the parish like a song.

'Twas Dreghorn brought the news to Manor – the ancient wooer. Wanlock broke a bottle of wine and made the occasion festival, but Mirren could not be discovered.

Full of his plans, her father went that evening to her chamber at an hour when she should be bedded, and found with apprehension that although the door was barred the chamber held no tenant. He went outside in darkness lashed by rain, and to her open window: made his way within – and found the brooch upon her unpressed pillow! It caught a flicker from the fire and shot a lance of light across the room.

"My God!" cried Wanlock harshly, "oh, my God! is this himself, Mahoun?" and with the jewel burning in his loof, he turned to see his daughter, with a face of shame and fear, framed in the open window. She had, in other hours, a sweetness and a charm like sunny Highland weather, or like the little lone birds of the sea, or like an air of youth remembered; but now arising from the outer night of misty exhalations, pallid against the background of the Manor trees, she seemed a blameful ghost.

He dragged her to his feet: as she knelt and cowered, he stamped with brutal passion on her fingers.

"Where have ye been?"

Her gallant spirit plucked her back from the edge of swound to which his cruel act had brought her: she looked without a tremor in his face, and the third blow fell when she told him she had been to Mellish.

"Mellish!" he cried aghast, "and, madam, what in the name of God have you to do with Mellish? He gave you this?" And he pressed with a brutal thumb the fateful gem against her parted lips so sore it seemed to shed its juices like a berry.

"I love him, and he has long loved me, and – "

"What! and there was the Glasfurd woman!"

"He had never loved her, or only thought so at the first, and the freedom she has given him has more than made amends for his poverty. Father, I am going to marry him."

"Mellish! A ruined man! And you know my pact with Dreghorn?"

"Your pact, father, but never mine: I should die first. It was the horrid prospect sent me to The Peel to-night. The thing is settled: he gave me his troth with the brooch you hold there in your hand – oh, the dear brooch! the sweet brooch of happy omen! – and you will let us marry, will you not? I would never marry wanting your consent."

"Then ye will never have it if the man is Mellish!" cried her father. He thundered threats: he almost wept entreaties: every scrap of his affection reft from her and centred now on his blackguard son, but the girl was staunch: that night he drove her from his door.

It was with huge dismay he came upon the gem a fortnight later on the floor of his girl's deserted chamber. This new appearance for a moment filled his soul with panic – it seemed the very pestilence that walks in darkness – and then he realised she must have left it on the night he sent her forth. With the assassin's heart and the family humour, that had not been confined to Lady Grace, he wrapped the jewel up and sent it as his wedding present to The Peel.

To his outcast daughter and the man who loved her he could have done no kinder act, for their marriage hung upon his giving to it something of his countenance, and this ironic gift of what to them was ever a talisman benign, came to relieve a piteous situation. Mirren loved, but she had made a promise not to wed without her father's willingness, and she was such that she should keep her promise though her life was marred.

With a light heart, then, did Mellish ride with the jewel in his pocket to the house in town where she had taken refuge, and gladly taking the gem as proof of her father's softening, she married the man of her desire.

"And now, goodwife," said Mellish, "I will go down to Manor and make peace."

"You will take our lucky amulet," she said, and she pinned it in his scarf, and he galloped with the gaiety of a boy through the fallen autumn leaves to the house of Wanlock.

It was as if he came from realms of morning freshness to some Terror Isle! Gloaming was come down upon that sad reclusive lowland country: the silvery fog which often filled the valley where the mansion lay, austere and old and lonely, gave to the natural dusk a quality of dream, an air of vague estrangement, a brooding and expectant sentiment. The trees stood round like sighing ghosts, and evening birds were mourning in the clammy thickets. Only one light burned in the impoverished dwelling; Mellish, through the open window where it beamed un-curtained, saw old Wanlock sunk in meditation with a Bible on his knees, and with a heart of pity left the saddle.

Oh God! that men should die within stark walls in ancient long-descended properties, without a comprehension of the meaning of the misty world!

He passed within the frowning arch and beat upon the knocker. The clangour rang through the dark interior: the night stood hushed, save for the inquiry of the howlets in the pines, the plunge of the Manor Burn, the drip of crisply falling perished leaves, and, far away upon the coast, the roaring of the sea. Pervaded by the spirit of the scene and hour, misgivings came to Mellish, in whose heart the night seemed all at once inimical, fantastic, peopled with incorporeal presences. He heard their mutter, heard them move with cunning footsteps; of a sudden, near at hand broke forth the dolorous utterance of a soul beseeching and forlorn. The dreary note, prolonged and dying slowly, seemed to roll in waves far out on shoreless seas of space, and Mellish, agitated, beat again upon the ponderous brass.

He heard the halting shuffle of feet within; the door was opened; Wanlock stood with a candle in the entrance. One glance only he gave to Mellish, and slammed the door in his face!

Abruptly from the crowding night round Mellish burst a peal of mad and mocking laughter!

For a moment fear, resentment, and disbelief warred in his brain for his possession: fear, being stranger there, was routed by an effort of the will; disbelief surrendered to his reason; he was left alone on the battlefield with anger. It swept with purple banners through the rally of his senses: drunk with passion, he tore from his breast the gem that had misled him to that hateful door, and flung it in by the open window, then leaped upon his horse and galloped furiously for home.

Wanlock, with the candle in his hand, stood for a moment listening in the passage, glad with venom. He heard the thud of hoofs die off in the distance of the avenue, then, with a shock that left him trembling, the ululation of his old familiar – that dreadful bittern call! It was to-night more sad than he had ever heard it, more imbued with hopeless longing, yet in some way through its desolation went a yapping note of menace and alarm.

He hurried to his chamber with a sense of something older than mankind: he set the candle on the table; turned with eagerness to lift the Book – the comforter, the shield, – and there between the open pages, on the final verses of the seventh Psalm, lay the accursed brooch!

It seemed to him like a thing that had come from the void outside the rim of human life where evils muster with black wings and the torments of men are fashioned. He whimpered as he made to seize it, then, as if it stung him, felt a numbness in the arm. Through his brain for a moment went the feeling of something gush: he staggered on the floor: a mist swept through his eyes. His vision cleared, and he saw the jewel at his feet. He bent to lift it with some curious failure in his members, groped with an impercipient hand, and found his fingers would not close upon it!

"My God!" he mumbled, "what is this come on me?" A mocking chuckle sounded through the room, and the final doubts of Wanlock vanished – another blow was come, and he was in the grip of the Adversary!

With his other hand he caught the gem, and rising slowly, cast a glance of wild expectancy about the room. No assurance came from the discovery that to the eye at least he was alone, yet a subtler sense than vision told him he had company, and he looked above him into the umber rafters, then turning to the window, saw enormous hands claw on the sill. They seemed to drag a weight from the nether world behind them: he watched them fascinated, even to the sinews' tension, till there raised and rested on the backs of them a face more horrible than he had ever dreamt of – blurred, maculate, amorphous! From the sallow visage peered inquiring eyes profound with cunning, and the soul of Wanlock grewed.

"We wrestle," he mumbled, "not against flesh and blood, but against principalities, against powers, against the rulers of the darkness": he seized upon the Book, and held it before him like a buckler, all his being drenched in the spirit of defiance, and he cried the Holy Name.

He cried it as they cried it on the moors – his people, when the troopers rode upon them: he cried with their conviction that the Blood had all things pacified, redeemed, and the apparition chuckled!

The last redoubt of Wanlock's faith surrendered: he madly wrenched a page from the sacred volume, crushed it with the jewel in his hand, and threw them in the face of his tormentor, then fell, a withered man, upon the bedstead, while the bittern cry outside arose in demon laughter.

When he drifted back from the bliss of his oblivion, he lay a while like a child that makes its world afresh each morning from a few familiar surrounding things – the light, the shade, the feel of textures, and the sound of the cinder falling on the hearthstone. All his life came ranked before him in epochs that grew more vivid as his brain grew clear – the folly of youth, the vanity of manhood, the pride of his strength, the dour determination of his will; but he saw them all as virtues. Had he not prayed, and sat at the Communion? Had he not felt the gust of the Holy Spirit? Had he not repented? – nay, penitence had been denied him from his very birth, and without repentance well he knew there was no sin's remission. Thus are the unelect at last condemned for a natural inability – terror they have and chagrin at results, but no regret for the essential wrong. There was a sound of some one moving in the house – the servant, who had been on a private escapade of her own, was now returned. Wanlock seized a walking-cane he kept beside the bedstead for the purpose, and he loudly rapped upon the wall. At first there was no answer; then he rapped again, and the woman entered, flushed with some spirit of adventure.

She had the radiant sleekness of the country's girls, – a strapping, rosy healthfulness, a jaunty carriage, and a dancing and inviting eye: she seemed to Wanlock for a moment like a stranger, and she carried with her scents of the cool night winds.

For a moment she looked at him, astounded – he had so suddenly grown very old and his mouth so strangely twisted; then she gave a little cry, and hurried to his bedside, and he saw that the shawl she wore was pinned upon her shoulder by the luckless brooch!

It glowed portentous and commanding like a meteor; with the squeal of a netted hare he grasped at his walking-cane, and struck with fury at the object of his terror. The woman shrank before the blow; the rattan swept the candle from the table to the floor: a fountain of flame from the hell that is under life sprang up the bedstead curtains!

With an oath old Wanlock staggered from his bed in time to save himself, but the Manor-house was doomed – at dawn the bitter smell of woody ashes blew across the valley.

From the shabby lodge-house midway in the avenue he looked astonished at the girdling hills, to see them all so steadfast and indifferent: the sun came up and sailed across the heavens, heedless of the smouldering space among the pines, where turret and tower more lofty than themselves had seemed, a day ago, eternal. The rat squeaked as it burrowed for a new home under fallen lintels; the raven croaked upon the cooling hearth. And night came down on these charred relics, swiftly – night, the old conquering rider, ally of despair! It appeared to Wanlock like a thousand years since he had had a careless heart, yet the ruin of his home for the moment seemed less dreadful than its cause, and the new light it had thrown on his situation. Never before was he so desolate, so desolate! – forsaken of God and man. All night his flaming house had stained the clouds: the crackle of its timbers and the thunder of its falling walls appeared to fill the whole world's ear, yet none had come to his assistance: as if abhorred by all, he was left to dree his weird alone among the ashes.

One thing only he had saved besides his life – a bottle of Bordeaux. He had seized upon it as the only friend from whom he could look for consolation. Even the maid and the dog had fled from him, but she returned at nightfall to the cheerless lodge to make it habitable.

"Where in the name of God got ye yon accursed thing?" he asked her, and she told him, flushing, she had got it from a lover.

"A lover!" quo' Wanlock, regarding his helpless arm, remembering happier things. "Are there still folk loving?"

"It's what he would like to be," said the woman awkwardly; "but the man's a dwarfish waif I daren't hardly venture through the woods for; ye'll have heard him screech for a month past. He haunts me like a bogle, comes from I kenna where – a crazy, crooked, gangrel body, worse than the Blednock brownie. He was squatted at the door last night when I got home, and he gave me the brooch, – I – I wish to the Lord I had never seen it."

"Where is it now?" asked Wanlock.

"I – I have given it back," the girl replied with some confusion.

"Ye were wise in that," said her master. "Woe upon the owner of the havock brooch! for I have had it too, and the heart of me is withered in my bosom. No brooch, no human brooch, I'll warrant! but a clot of the blood that dried on the spear of the Roman soldier. Ye have trafficked with the devil and have worn his seal. It has robbed me of my money and my home, my son, my daughter, and the power of my members – look at that blemished arm!"

She watched him for a moment, fascinated, seeing now his palsy; he beheld the pity in her eye, resenting it, and caught with his able hand at the bottle of Bordeaux, which he poured with a splash into a tarnished goblet. He was about to drink it when he saw a look of fear and speculation come upon her face.

"May the Lord forgive me, Manor!" she exclaimed, "but I gave the brooch this morning to your son!"

"To my son!" he cried, incredulous. "How could you have seen him? He is far from here."

"He never left the country," cried the woman, weeping "and I have known his hiding all the time. He saw the brooch upon me, was furious when he heard how I had got it, and made me give it up."

"Furious," said Wanlock curiously. "Had he the right?"

"None better," said the woman, looking on the floor.

"I might have guessed," said Wanlock bitterly. "'Though thou shouldst bray a fool in a mortar among wheat with a pestle, yet will not his foolishness depart from him.' He has the brooch! Then are his footsteps dogged by the Accuser of the Brethren, for the gem is hell's bellwether!"

The night was tranquil, windless, frosty-cold; deep in the valley's labyrinth lay the lodge-house, far from other dwellings, alien, apparently forgot, with the black plumes of the trees above it. In pauses of the conversation something troubled Wanlock like the fear of ambush, some absorbing sense of breathing shadows: silence itself took on a substance and stood listening at the threshold.

Suddenly there came a scratching at the door, and Wanlock blenched.

"God save us!" said the girl, and her face like sleet.

"I dare ye to open the door!" cried Wanlock, shaking.

"It is the dog," she said – "the dog come back; I left it in the company of Stephen."

"There is some compact here with things beyond me," said her master. "Open – open the door and see."

One glance only Wanlock gave at the grey dog trotting in, and fell to weeping when he saw a neckcloth pinned upon it with the brooch! He reeled a moment at the sight, then fumbled at the neckcloth and drew out the gem. With a curse he cast it in the heart of the burning peats, where it lay a little, blinking rubescent, then rolled among the cooler ashes. He moved expectant to the open door where the dog was leading: the girl took up the gem, which stung her like an asp upon the palm; she dropped it in the goblet, where it hissed and cooled among the wine, and at that moment rose the cry of Stephen in the avenue.

With a snatch at the burning candles she ran out behind her master, where he stood with head uplifted looking at the squadrons of the stars. She was the first to reach the figure lying on the ground, and putting down the candlesticks, she raised the lad, whose face was agonised and white like sapple of the sea. He had no eyes for them, but, trembling, searched with a fearful glance the cavern of the night made little by the candles burning in the breathless avenue.

"Stephen! Stephen! what has happened?" cried the girl, her lips upon his cheek.

"It – it caught me," gasped the lad. "I ran from The Peel, and it caught me, clawed upon my thrapple, and left me here. I pinned my neckcloth on the dog."

He leaned upon the woman, helpless in his terror. "Bring me the wine!" she bade her master, and old Wanlock stumbled back to fetch it.

"Oh, Stephen! Stephen! what were ye doing at The Peel?" she asked. "Ye know ye promised me – "

"I could not help myself," he answered, "knowing what was in the well. 'Twas that that kept me in the country. I got it out and was making off with it when I heard the eerie laugh again. I dropped the plunder at the very door of Mellish when the de'il was on me. He was no bigger than a bairn, but he kept upon my heels till I got here, and then he leaped."

"My Stephen! oh, my Stephen!" cried the woman, fondling him upon her breast, and he hung within her arms. A snarl came from the shadows: a creature smelling of mould and rotten leafage, clothed as in ragged lichens, contorted like a pollard willow, leaped at the throat of Stephen and crushed it like a paste, then fled with the bittern call.

Old Wanlock heard the woman shriek: he tottered with the goblet from the lodge and came within the circuit of the candles where she knelt beside her lover.

"He's gone! he's gone!" she cried, demented. "The devil has strangled him," and at the moment passed the ghost of Stephen Wanlock.

"I knew it," said the father – "very well I knew it: the sixth blow! There is no discharge in this war!" His head seemed filled with wool: his blood went curdling in its channels, and he staggered on his feet. Raising the goblet till it chattered on his teeth, he drained it at a draught, and the woman, heedless, straightened out the body of his son.

She heard her master choke: she turned to see his face convulsed, his eyeballs staring, and the empty flagon falling from his hand.

"The brooch! the brooch!" she screamed: a gleam of comprehension passed for a moment over Wanlock's purpling visage: he raised his arms, and stumbling, fell across the body of his son!

The First-foot

I

THE husband, with an eye of warm alacrity and a welcome manner that should have made his fortune in some livelier hostel than the dreary inn of Flanders Moss, regarded the stranger with compassion. The wife, an acrid peevish body, ill-content to be roused from bed at such an hour, plucked at the strings of her night-cap, loosened and fastened them half a dozen times as if they bridled a wroth that choked her, and looked with candid disapproval on the customer standing in the kitchen with the rain running from his wraprascal coat on the fresh-caumed flagstones of her floor.

"H'm!" she coughed; "it's no' a time o' the year when we're lookin' for many visitors to the Flanders Moss."

"But still-and-on ye're welcome," said the husband hastily, tender of the stranger's feelings. "I think there's an egg or twa, Jennet, isna there? And – and the hen; or – or yon ham?"

But Jennet tied her cap more tightly down upon her ears.

"I was making for the port o' Menteith," explained the stranger in a breath, compassing the chamber and the characters before him at a gled's glance, feeling himself master of them both, flinging off the wraprascal and throwing his bonnet on the hearth to dry. It struck the stone with a sodden slap that would have made plain the kind of night from which he had escaped, even if the ear had not more eloquently indicated that the house was in the very throat of tempest.

"Ye'll no hae pack nor powney?" said the dame sourly, with a pursed mouth, surveying the young man's hose, the clinging knee-breeches, the stained red waistcoat, and the shabby green cutaway coat, but more intent upon the dissipation of his shaven boyish countenance, the disorder of his hair, and his reckless eye.

"Tut, tut! It's no' a nicht for a cadger's dog, let alane a powney," said the amiable host; and then, in a beseeching tone that told the nature of their partnery, "Am I richt or am I wrang, Jennet? At least there maun be an egg or twa."

The wife scowled at her mate, and said emphatically that eggs were out of the question, and the hour was quite ridiculous.

"I'm no heedin'," said the stranger; "I had a meal of a kind at Fintry. What I want's a bed."

"Ye'll get that!" cried the landlord heartily, glad to be assured of a speedy return to his own blankets. "There's a snug bed ben, and ye'll hae a' the better appetite for breakfast."

"But what's your security?" demanded madam, and the goodman sighed.

Her customer shrugged his shoulders, threw himself in a chair, and thrust his feet out to the fire of turf.

"God," said he.

"Sir?" she queried.

"I said God was my security," remarked the stranger.

"Ye couldna hae better!" cried the innkeeper, and drawing a chopin of ale for the pious gentleman, beat down by the very gust of his geniality the rising opposition of the woman's manner.

Twenty minutes later Black Andy went to bed in the ben. He went with his boots on, for he had, in the very act of stooping to unlace them by the light of a tallow candle, seen that which led at the end to the rout of any thought of sleep. The candle, which he had placed on the floor the better to see his knots untied, threw a beam under a heavy oaken kist in the corner, and glinted on a ring of brass that oddly hung from the bottom of the box. He threw up the lid, to find no more than a pile of homespun blanketing; then turned the kist quietly on its side, to learn that the ring was on the latch of a secret bottom. He opened it: the shallow space between the false bottom and the real one seemed at first to hold no more than rags; but fumbling through them, he found a leather pouch with three-and-twenty guineas – madam's private hoard! As he counted the money silently on the covering of the bed, the storm that held the Flanders Moss in its possession seemed for the while to hold its breath, as he did his own, so that he could hear the thud of his heart and each reluctant tick of the kitchen clock.

For an hour he lay in darkness, wide awake, with the pouch in his breast. The murmur of voices in the kitchen ceased, its light went out; the lonely inn on the edge of the moor was black, and wholly lost in the privacy of the night.

The innkeeper, easy man! turned his face to the box-bed wall in the kitchen, and counted sheep going through a dip-tank till the fleece of the last of them spread, and spread, and spread, like a magic counterpane, and fell on him at last, smothering him to sleep. It was his goodwife's elbow. For she lay on her back, her hands hollowed behind her ears, her capstrings loose, and listened for some other sound than the creak of the roof-cabars, the whistle of the thatch, and tempest's all-pervading symphony. Ah! it would have been an easier night for her if she had had some chance to put her money elsewhere; it was her evil star that had surely brought this man to Flanders Moss on a Hogmanay, the very night when all honest bodies ought to be at their own fire-ends!

A sound in the room where he lay brought her sitting up in bed with every sense alert. A sash squeaked: she shook her husband out of the fleece of sleep, and they jumped together to the chamber door. It opened to a gale that blew right through it from an open window: their lodger was gone!

"I kent it!" cried the woman furiously, and shrieked to realise, by a feel of the hand in the dark, that her hoard had been discovered.

"Dod, now, that's droll!" said her husband, scratching his head. "And him had such good security!"

II

Black Andy, with the pouch of guineas comforting the breast of him like liquor, so that he hardly missed his wraprascal or his bonnet that were drying by the kitchen fire, ran along the broken road for Kippen. It was like the bed of a burn, and like a rested monster rose the storm afresh from the Hieland hills. One glance he gave behind him at a step or two from the window whence he burst; so dark was the night that the inn in the womb of it was quite invisible. He looked over his shoulder for a second time, having run for a little, and saw the bobbing of a lanthorn. His amiable host was already on his track, and Kippen was plainly no place for Black Andy.

With an oath he quitted the road, ran down through a clump of hazel, and launched on the rushy moss that (as the story goes) had once been a part of the sea that threshed on Stirling rock.

Like many another man, this scamp, unskilled in thievery, had no sooner escaped the urgent danger of arrest than he rued his impulsive fall to the temptation of a bag of clinking coins. He had drunk through an idle youth, and others had paid the lawing; he had diced and cheated; he had borrowed and left unpaid; he had sold bad cattle and denied his warrandice; he had lived without labour – all of which is no more different from theft than tipsyness is different from drunkenness. But hitherto he had stopped on the verge of crime denominate, and it was his mother's only glad reflection when the thought of his follies haunted her pillow. Had the temptation of the inn-wife's gold come to him on another night, and elsewhere, he could have turned the broad of his back on it, and mustered conquering hosts of fear and of expedience to his support; the misfortune was that it found him in a desperate hour. For a week he had been in a most jovial company with some Campsie lairds; he had spent the price of his father's horse to the last plack royally, as if he had been a bonnet-laird himself, and New Year's Day should have seen him back at Blaruisken with the price of the horse, or else it meant disaster. Even that consideration scarcely would have made a thief of him (as he thought now), but for the wife in the Moss of Flanders inn; she had so little deserved to be the sole possessor of such gold. A comely wife, a civil wife, a reasonably hospitable wife (as he argued with himself), might have kept her money on the doorstep, and he would have been the last to meddle with it; but this one deserved some punishment, and he was, in a fashion, Heaven's instrument. The husband – true, he was a kindly soul (and here the instrument of Heaven found his sophistry weak a little at the knees); but Black Andy had an intuition that the hoard was secret, even from the husband, and he guessed aright the wife would never report the actual nature of her loss.

He seemed the more contemptible a thief to himself, because in one particular he had blundered like a fool. For yonder, beiking before the innkeeper's fire, were his wraprascal and his bonnet – the first, at least, a clue to his identity. There was not another wraprascal than his own in his native parish; the very name of the coat had seemed too sinister for his mother, and the garment made him kenspeckle over half the shire. Though the folk in the inn of the Flanders Moss might never before have cast an eye on him, they had but to hang that garment on a whinbush at their door to learn his history from scores of passers-by.

Thinking thus – not any penitent in him, but the poltroon that is in all of us at the thought of discovery by the world of what we really are – the woman's money coldly weighed upon his bosom like a divot. By God! a rotten bargain had he made – to swap the easy mind of innocence for three days' drinking with numskull bonnetlairds in a Campsie tavern.

But the thing was done, with no remedy; there was nothing for it but to tramp home and meet his obligation to his father.

So busily did his mind engage with these considerations that the increase of the tempest for a little never touched his comprehension. He came to himself with a start at a stumble in a hag whose water almost reached his knees, and he realised that he was ignorant of the airt he moved to, and that the passion of the night was like to shake the world in tatters. The very moss below him seemed to quiver like a bog; no rush, no heather shrub, but had its shrieking share in the cacophony of that unco hour upon the curdled spaces of the ancient sea. Black Andy put out his cold-starved hand before his face, and peered for it in vain; it might have been a hand of ebony.

For hours he laboured through that windy desert, airting, as he judged by the wind, for the north, as far away as possible from the inn of his misdoing, and weariness seemed to turn his blood to spring-well water, and his flesh to wool, so that the earthly cushion of the hags in which he sometimes stumbled tempted him to lie and sleep. The last sheuch would have done his business if he had not, sitting on its edge, beheld a glimmer of light from a window. He dragged with an effort towards it, climbed a dry-stone dyke, and felt with his hands along the back of some dwelling which he took for a shepherd's hut, until he came upon the door.

Breathlessly he leaned his shoulder to it and loudly rapped.

"First-foot!" he heard a voice exclaim, and remembered it was the New Year's Day as the bolt shot back and he fell in the arms – of the innkeeper!

"Ye're back, my man!" cried the innkeeper's wife, with a face as white as sleet. "It'll be to pay your lodgin?"

"Tut, tut! never mind the lawin'. It's the New Year's Day, and here's your dram," said the genial landlord. "But, man, yon was a bonny prank to play on us! We thought ye were awa' wi' the wife's best blankets."

"But a lodgin's aye a lodgin'," said the wife nervously; and Andy laughed, knowing her perturbation.

"Here's the lawin'," he exclaimed, and banged her pouch of guineas in her hand. "Ye'll can count it later, and I'm awa' to my bed again. Were ye really feared I was gaein' to cheat ye?"

It was the innkeeper who answered; his wife was off with her hoardings.

"Not me!" he said. "I kent ye had Grand Security."

Isle of Illusion

I

MACDONNELL of Morar, on the summer of his marriage, and when the gladness of it was still in every vein, sailed his sloop among the Isles. He went from sound to sound, from loch to loch, anchoring wherever the fancy took his lady, and the two of them were seeking what no one ever found nor shall find – that last and swooning pang of pleasure the Isles in summer weather, either at dawn or dusk, seem always to promise to youth and love. At night they lay in bays in the dim light of the cool north stars, or in the flush of the sunken sun that made wine of the sea-waves, and the island cliffs or the sandy shores seemed populous with birds or singing fisher-people.

It was very well then with Morar.

His wife was still a girl. In the mornings, when she came on deck with her hair streaming and the breeze making a banner of her gown, her gaiety surging to her breast in song, she seemed to him and to his men like one of the olden sea princesses told about in Gaelic stories, born from foam for the happiness and hurt of the hearts of men. She was lovely, tender, and good, and he himself, with those that knew him best, was notable for every manly part. One thing only he had a fear of in his bride – that, as had happened with others before, and perhaps with himself, a day might come to him when the riddle of her would be read, her maidenly sweet mystery revealed; when he could guess with certainty what was in the deep dark wells of her eyes, and understand, without a word, the cause for every throb of her bosom. To have her for ever with a part to baffle and allure, as does the sea in its outer caves, and as do the dawns in Highland glens – that was the wish of Morar.

The captain of the yacht, who, having no passion for her, knew her, some ways, better than her husband, perhaps, said she had what, westward in the Barra Isle he hailed from, they call the Seven Gifts for Women – content and gentleness, looks and liking, truth, simplicity, and the fear of God. To him and to his men – gallant fellows from Skye, and somewhat jealous of her that she was not of the Isles herself, but a stranger – she was at least without a flaw. One time they thought it might be temper was her weakness, for she walked the deck with pride and had a noble carriage of

47

the head, but the tiniest cloud of temper never crossed her honeymoon. Indeed, it was well with Morar.

And it seemed that summer as if the very clime befriended him, for there never blew but the finest breezes, and the sun was almost constant in the sky. Round all the remoter isles they sailed – even Harris and the Uists, and the countless lesser isles that lie to the west of Scotland, – an archipelago where still are dwelling the ancient Gaelic gods, whereto at least they come at sunset and sit upon the sands communing, so that sailors knowing the language, and having the happy ear, can sometimes catch far off at sea deep murmurs of the olden world that others take for the plash of waters.

Morar's wife put the yacht into every creek. She loved the little creeks, she doted on the burns going mourning through the darkness, and on the sound of tides on shallow shores; it was her great delight sometimes to sleep on land below a canvas shelter, bathe at morning in the inner pools, walk barefooted on the sand, or stand on rocky promontories facing the rising sun, with her hair tumultuous. Her first breakfast then was the wild berry, her morning drink the water from island wells.

"I could live on the berries," she would say to her husband. "Oh, I love them!"

"Doubtless, mochree," would he answer her, laughing. "Faith! it's my notion they have been growing all these years in the islands waiting just for you; their bloom is on your cheek; it's the berry stain that was on your lips since ever I knew you. But for a common person like myself there is a certain seduction in a sea-trout or a herring. Madam, I wish you joy of your wild berries, and indeed I love the taste of them – on your lips, – but let me press on you a simple cabin-biscuit, though it suffers from having been baked by the hand of man."

"And the berry comes straight from God," would be her answer. "It's the fruiting of the clean wild wind; I sometimes think that if I could eat it always I should live for ever."

"Then, faith, I'll grow it in Morar garden by the pole, and you shall eat berries at every meal," said her husband.

"Perhaps I'll acquire the taste myself. Meanwhile, let me recommend the plain prose of our cooking galley."

"And I declare that I can find in pure water something as intoxicating as wine and far more subtle on the palate."

"A noble beverage, at least they tell me so, as the piper says in the story," said Morar, "yet God forbid that a too exclusive diet of berries and water should send Macdonnell back a widower to Morar! I take leave to help you to another egg," and so saying he would laugh at her again, and she would laugh also, for the truth was that she never brought to the cabin table but a yachtsman's appetite.

One thing she missed in all these island voyagings was the green companionship of trees. She came from a land of trees, and sailing day after day past isles that gave no harbour to so little as a sapling, she fretted sometimes for the shady deeps of thicket and the sway of boughs. Often she sat on deck at nightfall and imagined what the isles must have been before disaster overtook them.

"Can you think of us wandering in the avenues, sitting in the glades? Barefoot or sandal, loose light garments, berries and water, the bland sea air, shade from the sun and shelter from the shower, and the two of us always young and always the same to each other" – it was a picture she put before him many times, half entranced, as if she once had known a life like that before far back in another age and climate than in Scotland of the storms. Kissing her lips, wet from some mountain well, her husband got to look on her now and then as some Greek girl of the books, and himself as an eternal lover who had heard the wind blowing through boughs in Arcady.

Loving trees as she did, it was strange that so long they should have failed to visit Island Faoineas, for often in their voyagings it lay before them on the sea – green, gracious, and inviting, its single hill luxuriant with hazel-grown *eas* or corrie, its little glen adorned with old plantations. It lies behind Bernera, south of Harris, hiding coy among other isles and out of the track of vessels, and for reasons of his own the captain of the yacht sailed always at a distance from it, keeping it in the sun's eye so that its trees should seem like black tall cliffs with the white waves churning at their feet. But one day Morar and his wife came to him with the chart. "This island here," they said together. "We have not seen it close at hand; let us go there to-night."

The captain's face changed; he made many excuses. "A shabby, small place," he told them, "with a poor anchorage. And the wind is going westward with the sun. I think myself Lochmaddy better for an anchoring this night than Ealan Faoineas."

"What does the name mean – this Ealan Faoineas?" asked Morar's wife, looking out toward the island that was too distant yet to show its trees.

"It means," said Morar, "the Isle of Seeming – that is to say, the Isle of Illusion."

"What a dear name!" she cried, clapping her hands. "I should love to see it. Are there trees?" Her eyes were on the captain's face: he dared not lie.

"What you might be calling a sort of trees," he grudgingly admitted. "Oh yes, I will not be saying but what there are two or three trees, or maybe more, for I have not paid much attention to Ealan Faoineas myself."

"Indeed!" said she. "Then it is time you were amending your knowledge of it. I think we will risk the anchorage for the sake of the trees."

It was her own hand put down the helm and herself who called the men to the sheets, for the captain had a sudden slackness in his office and was forward murmuring with his crew.

"What ails him?" the lady asked her husband.

"You have me there!" he answered her, as puzzled as herself. "I think it is likely there may be some superstition about the island; the name suggests as much, and now that I come to think of it, I remember I once heard as a boy that sailors never cared to land on one or two of the Outer Isles, believing them the domain of witchcraft. We must have passed that island frequently and the captain always kept us wide of it. I will ask him what its story is that makes him frightened for it."

He went forward by-and-by and talked with the captain.

"I am a plain man; I have not the education except for boats," said the seaman, "and I would not set foot on Faoineas for the wide world. You will not get a man in all the Outer Islands, from Barra Head to the Butt of Lewis, who would step on Faoineas if the deck of his skiff was coming asunder in staves below the very feet of him. I am brave myself – oh yes! I come of people exceeding brave and notable for deeds, but there is not that much gold in all the Hebrides, no, nor in the realm of Scotland, would buy my landing in that place yonder."

"Come! come! what is wrong with the island that you should have such a fear of it?" asked Morar, astounded at so strong a feeling.

"It is bad for men, and it is worse for women," said the captain.

"Is it something to hurt the body?"

"If it was but the body I would be the first ashore! I have not so much money put past me that I have any need to be afraid for my life," said the captain.

"Are there ghosts there, then?" said Morar, determined to be at the root of the mystery.

"Ghosts!" cried the captain. "Where are they not, these gentlemen?"

By this time the sloop that Morar's wife was steering had drawn closer on the island, breaking her way among the billows striving into Harris Sound; and to the gaze of Morar's wife, and to her great bewilderment, she saw the little glen with its bushes climbing high on either side of it, and the tall, great, dark old Highland trees beyond, and thickets like gardens to the south, and under all the deep cool dusk of shadows she had longed for all those days that she and her husband had sought for the last pang of pleasure in their honeymoon among the Outer Isles. She leaned upon the tiller and stared entranced and unbelieving, for it seemed a fairy isle, such as grows fast in dreams and sinks to the sea-depths again when dawn is on the window. Only when she saw rooks rise with cawings from the branches, and heard the song of birds unknown on the treeless islands, was she altogether convinced of its reality.

"Darling," she cried to her husband, "look! Were we not right? Here's a forgotten paradise."

"If paradise it be, then may you have your share of it," said the captain as he put them ashore. "Myself, I would not risk it so long as this world has so many pleasant things to be going on with. All I can tell you of Island Faoineas is that, paradise or purgatory, it depends on what one eats and drinks there. I heard it from a priest in Eriskay, a noble and namely man through all the islands of the West. Once he had landed here and known some wonders. He died in Arisaig, and in his dying blessed with the seven blessings one well upon this island, but which of all that run there I never learned."

That night Morar and his bride slept out in the shelter of hazel-bushes and shelisters. They built a fire and drank out of the same glass from a burn that sang through the shelisters, and as they slept there were many wells that ran merrily through their dreams, but one particularly that rose from a hillock beside them, and tinkled more sweetly than golden jewels streaming down a golden stair.

II

She was the first to waken in the morning, and stealing softly from him, she left the embers of their fire among the rushes and went wandering among the trees, so that when he rose he saw her figure, airy and white, among their columns. She seemed the spirit of the trees to his doting eye, as though 'twas there among them she had always dwelt; the wood was furnished and completed by her presence.

"There is not in the world a sweeter place," she cried, "and I have never seen such berries! Look, I have brought you some, Sir Sluggard, that we might taste them first together." She put a spray of the berries between her teeth and let him sweeten the fruit with a kiss as he took his share from her lips with his own.

"The woman tempted me, and I did eat," said Morar, laughing, and culled the berries with his arms around her. They burst on his palate with a savour sharp and heady. He was about to ask for more when he saw her change. The smile had suddenly gone from her face at his words; for the first time he saw that her eyes were capable of anger.

"Upon my word," said she in an impatient voice, "I think it a poor compliment to me after my trouble in getting the berries for you that you should have such a thought in your head about me."

"There you go," he answered quickly, an unreasonable vexation sweeping through him in a gust. "Did ever any one hear the like, that because I am indifferent to your silly berries you should snarl like a cat?"

"A cat!" she cried, furious.

"Just a cat," he repeated deliberately. "For God's sake give me peace, and get your hair up before the men come ashore for us. It is time we were home; I am heart-sick of this sailing. And it ill becomes a woman of your years to play-act the child and run barefoot about island sands."

The berries she still held in her hand she crushed between her palms till the juice of them stained her gown and ran like blood between her fingers.

The perfume rose to her nostrils and seemed to fill her head with a pungent vapour.

"Well? Well?" he said with irritation at her staring. She covered her eyes with her hands and burst into tears.

He only whistled. Someway she appeared a sloven in dress, awkward in gesture, and a figure of insincerity. If he had not a sudden new conviction that she was everything she should not be, there was the accent of her voice, the evidence of his eyesight. For when, in wild exasperation at his manner, she took her hands from her face, she showed a visage stained and sour, tempestuous eyes, and lips grown thin and pallid.

"I hate you! I hate you!" she cried, and stamped with her bare feet on the sand. "I cannot for my life understand what I ever saw in you that I should have married you. Any one with her senses might have hesitated to tie herself for life to a man with so much evil in his countenance."

"Yours would be none the worse for washing," said Morar remorselessly, with an eye on her berry-stained face.

"There's a gentleman!" she cried. "Oh, my grief, that I should have spoiled my life!"

"You knew what I was when you took me," said Morar. "Lord knows, I made no pretence at angelic virtues, and 'twas there, by my faith, I was different from yourself!"

"And there's the coward and liar too!" cried his wife. "You were far too cunning to show me what you really were, and it must have been a woeful ignorance of the world that made me take you on your own estimate."

"Well, then, the mistake has been on both sides," said Morar. "There's no one could be more astonished than myself that my real wife should be so different from what till this hour I had imagined her. Madam, you need not be so noisy; if you scream a little louder the crew will be let into a pretty secret. It is like enough they know you already, for I have been singularly blind."

He put up what seemed to her for the first time an unlovely hand to stifle a forced yawn: she saw an appalling cruelty in the mouth that had so often kissed her and called her sweet names; his very attitude expressed contempt for her.

"What have I done?" she asked, distracted.

"It is not what you have done," he said with a coarse deliberation, "'tis what you are and what you cannot help being. The repentance must lie with me. I would give, gaily, ten years of my life to obliterate the past six months."

"Faith, 'tis a man of grace and character says so to his newly-married wife."

At these words Morar started slightly, and looked for a moment confused. "Newly married!" he said; "Lord help us! so we are. Some way, I fancied we had been married for years. Well, we have not taken long to discover each other, and will have the more leisure to repent. I understand you, madam, into the very core; there is not a vein of your body hides a secret from me. I was mistaken; I thought your beauty something more than a pink cheek; I thought you generous till I saw how generous you could be at my expense, and how much the rent-roll of Morar weighed with you in your decision to marry me. I thought you humble and unaffected, and now I see you posing about this business of bare feet on the sand, the morning breeze in your gown, breakfasts of berries and water."

"Pray go on," cried the lady. "Pray go on. Every word you say confirms the character I now see in your face."

"I thought you truthful, so you are – in the letter and the word; but the flattery you have for those you would conciliate, the insincerity of your laugh in the presence of those you would please, the unscrupulousness of your excuses for the omission of duties unpleasant to you – what are these but lies of the worst kind?"

"Oh heavens," she cried, "I was not always so! If I am so now I must be what you made me. I remember – " she drew her hand across her brow; "I seem to remember some one else I thought was me, that loved you, and could not be too good and pure for you even in her imagination. You seemed a king to that poor foolish girl's imagination; she loved you so – she loved you so, she was so happy!"

"Just so!" said Morar. "You had, seemingly, well deceived yourself. And now I can tell you that you may cry your eyes out, for I know what a woman gets her tears so readily for. It is that when she is crying and lamenting she may not betray her chagrin and ill-temper in her face. Have done with it, and let us get out of this! I see the men put out the boat; they will be with us in a moment; for Heaven's sake let us have no more theatricals. The fate of us both is sealed, and we must, I suppose, live the rest of our lives together like the other married fools we know – putting as fair a face as we can on a ghastly business."

She was standing beside tall blades of shelister – the iris of the isles – and when he spoke like this to her she suddenly plucked a handful and began to tear them wantonly with her fingers.

"I assure you that you have seen the last of my tears," said she. "I would not cry out if you struck me! There is something almost as sweet as love, and that is hate, and I seem to have come from a race that must have either. I have a feeling in me that I could have loved eternally if I had found the proper object, but now I know that I can always be sure you will keep me hating, and I am not sorry. Yes, yes, you have said it, Morar, a ghastly business; but I will not put any fair face on it to deceive the world, I assure you! It could not be deceived: blind would it be, indeed, if it could not see the sneer in your face, and hear the coward in your voice."

"Silence, you fool; the men are coming!" he said, clutching at her wrist and twisting it cruelly.

She gave a little shriek of pain, and caught at her breast with the other hand that held the broken blades of shelisters.

"Oh, you have struck me!" she cried. "That is the end of my shame, and I shall make you suffer."

He saw a poignard glint momentarily in the morning sun that was turning Isle Faoineas' sands to gold, and before he could prevent her she had plunged the weapon in her bosom. She fell with a cry at his feet, her hair in the ashes of the fire they had last night sat by. The blood came bubbling to her mouth and welled out on her bosom where the poignard rose and fell with her moaning.

For a moment, instead of pity and remorse, there was a feeling of release. Behind him sounded the plash of oars; he turned hastily and saw the men had left the sloop and were approaching land. "Oh *Dhia!*" he said to himself, "here's a bonny business to explain!" and then 'twas very far from well with Morar, for he heard the woman moan her wish for water, and he knew she shared the agony of that inward fire that scorched his throat as if the berries he had swallowed had been beads of heated metal. At his feet was the glass they had drank from on the last night of their happiness; he picked it up and ran to the well that tinkled on the hillock, then hurried to her side and raised her up to let her drink.

The draught, it seemed, revived her; she shuddered and sighed, and turned in his arms; then his own torment mastered him, and he drank too.

Through his whole flesh went a pleasant chill; a gladness danced in him, and he saw a thing miraculous in his bride – the flush come back to her cheek, and all her wild sweet beauty, and her smile, as she leaned against his shoulder like one new waked from sleep, so that he looked into her face and saw himself reflected in her eyes. The berry stains were on her lips, the bosom of her gown was reddened with their juices, and in between her breasts lay the blade of the shelister, sparkling with dew, and glinting in the sunshine as it rose and fell in time with her heart's pulsations.

"Oh, love!" she said, and put her arms about his neck, "I dreamt – I dreamt a dreadful dream!"

"And I, sweetheart," said Morar, looking aghast at the berry stains, and the mark of his fingers on her wrist, and on the iris blade that were evidence it had been no dream. "I dreamt, too, love – my God! such dreaming! I do not wonder now the world holds far aloof from this Island of Illusion. God bless the well, the holy well; but the curse of curses on the berries of Ealan Faoineas!"

Together, hand in hand, they fled to the shore and waded out on the sandy shallow to meet the boat; the sloop shook out her sails like some proud eager bird; from her deck, together waist-encircled, they saw the blue tide rise on the yellow sands, the trees nod, the birds flit among the thickets of the glen, and heard the tinkle of the well in Ealan Faoineas.

The Tudor Cup

I

WHEN the Tudor Cup was sold at Sotheby's in the year 18— for the sum of £7000, the fall of the auctioneer's hammer echoed round the world – at all events, round the world of men who gather bibelots. There were only three such treasures in existence – this one now destined for America, which was understood to have come from Holland; another in the national collection in Paris; and a third in Scotland, the property of Sir Gilbert Quair, whose ancestor had acquired it one hundred and fifty years before by winning a game of cards in a London coffee-house.

Among those people who were profoundly moved by this record price for a quite unimpressive-looking battered silver tankard was the firm of Harris & Hirsch, the Bond Street art-dealers; and two days after the sale in London, Mr Harris hastened up to Scotland, quartered himself at an inn in Peebles, and pushed some discreet inquiries. Sir Gilbert Quair, he discovered, was in a state approaching penury, living an almost hermit life in the House of Quair beside the Tweed, with a deaf old housekeeper, a half-daft maid who never came out-of-doors, and an equally recluse man whose duty it was to act as guide to the numerous tourists who flocked to the house for the sake of its place in Ballad Minstrelsy and its antiquarian collection. If the gossips of Peebles could be trusted, the baronet lived upon the shilling fees his guide exacted from the visitors, dodging, himself, from room to room of his mansion for fear of encountering Americans and English, whom he hated – resenting their intrusion on his privacy, but counting their numbers eagerly as from his window he watched them coming up the long yew avenue.

Harris, the Bond Street dealer, modestly bent on hiding his own importance in the commercial world of art – for the nonce a simple English gentleman with a taste for miniatures – called next day at the House of Quair, whose crenellated tower looked arrogantly over ancient woods and fields where lambs were bleating piteously and men were walking along the furrows scattering seed.

The avenue of yews, which led from the highway into Peebles through neglected and dishevelled grounds, brought the Bond Street dealer to the forlorn façade of the mansion and the great main door. He rapped upon the iron knocker; the sound reverberated as through a vault, with hollow echoes such as come from vacant chambers. Far back in the dwelling's core there was a clatter of something fallen, but no one answered to the summons of the visitor; and having rapped in vain again, he ventured round the westward wing, to find himself confronted by a door on the side of which was hung the evidence that this was properly his entrance. It was a painted board, with the legend –

QUAIR COLLECTION.

Open to the Public Tuesdays and Thursdays.

ADMISSION ONE SHILLING

Now this was neither a Tuesday nor a Thursday, and Harris swore softly. He was just on the point of making his retreat when a footstep sounded on the gravel of a little walk that led to a bower upon the terrace, and turning, he found himself face to face with Sir Gilbert Quair.

"The collection is not on view to-day, sir," said the baronet, an elderly thick-set gentleman wearing a shabby suit of tweed.

Mr Harris took off his hat – not to the wearer of the shabby tweed suit, but to the owner of the Tudor Cup.

"I am most unfortunate," he stammered. "I was not aware that the collection was only on view on certain days, and, unhappily, I must return to England this evening. It happens that I am something of an amateur in miniatures, fortunate in the possession of a few choice examples, and, being in this neighbourhood, I could not resist the temptation to see the celebrated collection of Sir Gilbert Quair, which is rich in miniatures."

He passed the baronet his card, to which the name of a well-known London club contributed the proper degree of uncommercial importance. Sir Gilbert turned it over in his fingers with a little hesitation, shot a shy glance of the keenest scrutiny from under his bushy eyebrows at the visitor.

"In the circumstances –" he began, and taking a key from his pocket, unlocked the door which led to the collection, but before he let his visitor through he held out to him a little wooden box with a slit in the lid of it. "In the absence of the usual guide," said he, "I'll collect your shilling for him, Mr Harris."

Five minutes later Harris was manifesting the most rapturous appreciation of Sir Gilbert's miniatures, which in truth were nothing wonderful; but at every opportunity, when unobserved by his host, his eyes went ranging in search of the Tudor Cup. It was his host who finally called attention to it under glass in a corner cupboard.

"If you had been interested in old English silver, Mr Harris, this piece might have had some attraction," said Sir Gilbert, drenching his flaring nostrils with a pinch of snuff from a tiny ivory spoon. "I'm no great judge myself, but my father highly prized it."

The Bond Street dealer, with a thudding heart, peered through the glass at the very counterpart of that tarnished goblet which had fetched £7000 in Sotheby's. He was wondering if the dry, old, shabby gentleman looking over his shoulder, and odorous with macconba, was aware that this was a Tudor Cup, or if he had read the newspapers carefully and knew what Tudor Cups were worth in Sotheby's.

II

"But Himmel! did you not make him an offer?" demanded Hirsch next day in the Bond Street shop – they called it gallery – to which his partner had returned from Tweedside with the profound depression a man might have who had for a fleeting moment seen the only woman he could ever love and then had lost her in a panic.

"Offer, Joel!" he replied in accents of despair. "I offered him five thousand, and he only chuckled. He would not even take it from the cupboard. 'No, no, Mr Harris,' he said with his head to the side, flicking up his abominable snuff; 'it is an heirloom older than any here, and I am not selling.' And the galling thing is that he doesn't even know he has a Tudor Cup, nor what a Tudor Cup can fetch in Sotheby's."

"Ah, you should have had the money with you, Harris," said his partner. "Always show the money, I say; it talks for you through a speaking-trumpet. By heavens, I will go myself to Scotland and have that Tudor Cup, if I have to steal it!"

III

A spirit of romance and a solemn homily on mutability were in the scene when Hirsch walked into the grounds of Quair, though he was not the man to understand. Six hundred years of history cried from the old bastion; still in its shelter men sowed oats, and their shabby dwellings clustered, no way changed, to look at, since the Borderland was vexed with wars and Quair was lord and warden; but vassals no more, save to that grim seigneur Commerce, who took from them triple-tithes and children instead of the service of the sword, which was all the old lords claimed. A valley of peace, and nights untroubled, and the old bold fighting Quairs in their resting graves, and their troopers' dust at the roots of English pastures; surely at eve in the woods of Quair, or riding spirit horses through the passes of the hills, a thousand ghosts went seeking lost passions, old delights.

It was Thursday afternoon. Hirsch stepped in at the door which led to the Quair Collection, to find the man in charge of it had all the customary cicerone's dull loquacity. He dribbled dates and gushed details of family history as if he were a gargoyle who had never got refreshment from the currents pouring through him. Thick-set, short, and rasped upon the chin from too-close shaving, he looked the very figure of a man to fill one of the empty suits of mail that flanked the entrance to the gallery, and even to the shopman's eye of Hirsch he had an air of truculence that somehow seemed to accord with the situation.

"You do not appear to have many visitors to-day," said the picture-dealer, having looked perfunctorily at dingy tapestry and pictures, and now with eyes, in which the fires of covetousness were with difficulty restrained, upon the tarnished Tudor Cup in its corner cupboard.

"Ye're the first this week," said the guide with acerbity, as if the shilling fees were a more personal matter than the gossips of the countryside believed; and Hirsch the dealer, rubbing his hook-nose to conceal the tremulous avidity of his mouth, saw that disappointed avarice was in this creature's eyes.

"I should like, a little later on, to see Sir Gilbert," said the dealer, who had five thousand pounds in his pocket, and a Jew's conviction that an impecunious Scot could never resist the delicious crackle of English notes.

"Ye canna; he's from home," explained the guide. "He's awa' to Edinburgh for a month."

A thought came there and then to the dealer which made him pale. Avarice and cunning were in the old man's face; his shillings plainly meant a lot to him; his clothing was in poor accord with the guardianship of treasure.

"Look here," said Hirsch in a confidential whisper. "If your master is to be away for a month, there is no reason why the matter I meant to arrange with him should not be arranged with you, and put a handsome sum of money in your pocket. I have taken a fancy to this silver jug, and though I know Sir Gilbert will not part with it, I thought he might at least agree to let me have it copied. It's a thing that is often done, Mr –"

"Meldrum," said the guide with a promising air of equanimity.

"In two or three weeks I could have my copy made in Paris, and this cup returned to you in safety, and no one else except ourselves need be a bit the wiser, Mr Meldrum."

The guide gave a laugh that was half a sneer, and checked it suddenly with a hand upon his mouth. "It's a maist singular proposition," he remarked reflectively. "In the four-and-twenty years I have been showin' folk the Quair Collection I havena heard the like of it. And it comes from a total stranger!"

"I represent one of the most reputable firms in London," Hirsch hastened to explain, with the simultaneous production of his business card.

Meldrum looked at it with interest. "Harris & Hirsch. I take it that you are Mr Hirsch? There was a Mr Harris calling on Sir Gilbert, I was tell't, some days ago."

"Exactly," answered Hirsch. "My partner. He had almost completed negotiations for the loan of the cup for the purpose I have mentioned. But really there seems no need for us to be troubling Sir Gilbert. The cup will be back before his return from Edinburgh, and –"

"Just that!" said Meldrum dryly. "And what about my security?"

Delighted with such apparent pliability, Hirsch produced his English notes, which brought a very passion of greed to Meldrum's eyes.

"Let us not be calling it security, Mr Meldrum," he remarked insidiously. "If a hundred pounds – "

Again the guide ironically chuckled. "If I could trust ye for a hundred pounds, Mr Hirsch, I could trust ye mair for ten times that," he said. "I take your word for't that we needna ca't security: if I'm to risk my job and my reputation, the cost of three weeks loan o' that siller tankard is exactly a thousand pounds!"

. . .

Three weeks later, the Quair Cup and its duplicate came back from Tregastel of Paris, so much alike that Hirsch would have been beat to see a difference had it not been that he found on one a private microscopic mark he had put on it himself.

But it was not the cup so marked that he returned to the accommodating Meldrum.

Two months more, and the curio world was shaken once again by the intimation of another Tudor Cup for sale at Sotheby's. Amongst the host of possible bidders who examined the precious piece of tarnished metal taken out impressively from Sotheby's strongest safe some days before the sale, was Barraclough, the expert who had bought its fellow earlier in the season for his client in America.

"A brilliant forgery," he exclaimed on careful scrutiny – "one of Jules Tregastel's charming reproductions," and departed.

Harris & Hirsch were sent for by the auctioneer. "Nonsense!" they protested – and Hirsch satisfied himself again that the microscopic mark of the veritable cup from Quair was there. "Tregastel never had a tool on it."

"Hadn't you better ask?" said the auctioneer, and they asked by telegram, with astounding consequences.

"The cup you sent was a copy made a year ago by myself for another client. I thought you knew," replied Tregastel.

"Mein Gott!" cried Harris, appalled. "Tregastel has made so cunning a job of it he has even copied your private mark, and you have sent the original back to Quair."

"I will not believe it! I will not believe it!" said his partner, almost weeping with chagrin.

That night the two of them went to Scotland, and in the morning Harris went out from Peebles to the House of Quair to see Sir Gilbert.

"Might I have another look at the cup?" he asked without periphrasis, and the baronet snuffed and chuckled.

"It seems to have wonderfully taken your fancy, Mr Harris," he remarked with an ironic cough. "Again you are unfortunate in the day you call, for this is Wednesday. And in any case I thought I made it clear that the cup was bound to stay here in spite of your most tempting offers."

"I know," replied the dealer; "but I should like to see it – that is all."

"Ah! you mad collectors!" said Sir Gilbert humorously. "Ye can be as crazy over a bashed old siller cup as I might have been mysel' at one time over a bonny lassie! Well, come your ways in and you shall see it. It is aye another shillin'!"

Harris not only saw the cup, but this time got it into his hands. In a fever of apprehension he turned it up and down and sought for a microscopic mark like that which Hirsch had pointed out upon the other, – it was not there!

At the sight of the blank look on his face Sir Gilbert chuckled and took snuff. "I see you have discovered, Mr Harris," he remarked with his eyebrows twitching. "You connoisseurs are not to be deceived so easily!"

"Then – then you know it is a forgery!" cried Harris with amazement.

"I would not use that word for it exactly, Mr Harris," said the baronet with a gesture of distaste. "A copy – and a wonderful copy too, by Tregastel of Paris. The truth is, I sold the original some months ago in London, having first had this one made. You see my possession of a Tudor Cup is notorious, and if it got about that the Quair Collection was being in any way depleted, where would our shillin's come from, Mr Harris?" and he jocosely poked his visitor in the ribs.

Harris flew back to the inn at Peebles, an object of unutterable despair.

"Mein Gott! these Scotch!" cried Hirsch, wringing his hands. "But I will have my money back from that Meldrum man if I have to take him to the courts."

"Harris & Hirsch would cut a funny figure in the courts in the circumstances, Joel," said his partner. "It is better that we go out together to-morrow, when your Meldrum's place is open, and compromise."

The entrance to the Quair Collection had been hardly opened on the morrow when the dealers tried to push their way within. Harris was perturbed when he saw who checked them on the threshold – Sir Gilbert Quair himself, who greeted him with a crafty smile, only a little shabbier in dress than when he had seen him hitherto, and with the box for the admission shillings hanging round his neck.

"It might be the flowin' bowl, Mr Harris," he exclaimed ironically. "Ye come back so often to it."

"I want a word or two with you," said Mr Hirsch peremptorily, finding the old man barred their further passage. "Did you know that cup you lent me was an imitation?"

"I could hardly fail to be aware of it," said the baronet. "You surely didna think a paltry thousand pounds would be security for a genuine Tudor Cup, and a' the world sae keen on them at Sotheby's."

"I have been deceived; I must have my money back!" said Hirsch, and the old man shrugged his shoulders and took snuff.

"Na, na!" he said. "A bargain's aye a bargain, and ye canna get your money back. The best I can dae for ye is to swop the cup ye sent for the one I lent ye."

"Look here, Meldrum —" Hirsch began, and Harris, with surprise, corrected him.

"Not Meldrum," he remarked. "Sir Gilbert Quair."

"Ye're both of ye right, and ye're both of ye wrang," said the old man with a chuckle. "For twa years back I've been guide to my own collection; it's the only way to keep an eye upon the shillin's."

"You d – d old rogue!" exclaimed the partners simultaneously, and he grinned at them, with his stout old breast across the doorway like a cliff. For a little he gloated on their fury, then took them by the arms and led them out upon the terrace.

"You see this land," he said, and indicated all the hills and valleys, verdant woods and furrowed fields, and the river sounding at the bend below the mansion. "The greed of English thieves brought them here marauding for good six hundred years, and it seems ye're no done yet! My forefolk fought you with the sword, but Gilbert Meldrum Quair must fight you with his wits!"

"But, Gott in Himmel! we are not English; we are Hebrews!" protested Hirsch with his hands palm upwards and his neck contracted.

"That is worse," replied Sir Gilbert, making for his door. "We Scots are still at feud wi' the Jews for what they did out yonder in Jerusalem."

"Copenhagen": A Character

WHEN I go home on summer visitations, old friends, with the most generous desire to aid one in an eccentric and indeed half-daft and wholly disreputable way of living, come to me covertly in reckless moments "for auld lang syne," and remind me of native characters ancient or modern. They themselves are (if they only knew it) characters the most superb for any of my purposes, but, wholly unsuspecting, they narrate the whims and oddities, the follies and conceits of others, lamenting always that the race of characters is rapidly running done. "When Jiah, and Jocka, and Old Split-a-dale are gone," say they, "we'll can take to reading your own bits of stories, for there'll be nothing better left to do, and not a ploy from Martinmas to Whitsunday and back again."

I know better, of course. I know that unconventional characters – fantastic, whimsical, bombastic, awkward, crazed – will come to the surface there and elsewhere as constant as the bracken comes upon the braes in spring.

But age, undoubtedly, whether it matures an oddity or not, endears him to you if yours be the proper sympathetic soul for such caprices of the stars. What in a droll "going-about body" of thirty seems a rogue's impertinence will appear to some one else, thirty years after this, or even to yourself perhaps, a quaint wit, and his sayings and doings will be the cause of merriment over all the countryside. So it is that even I am sometimes constrained to think the old characters dead and gone will never have such brilliant successors.

I had that thought yesterday as I walked past Copenhagen's school. Alas! not Copenhagen's school, for Copenhagen wields no earthly ferrule, and lies with many of his pupils under grass in Kilmailie, and the little thatched academy, where we drowsed in summer, and choked in winter in the smoke of our own individual peats, is but a huddle of stones, hidden by nettles, humbled in the shade of the birch-tree from which old Copenhagen culled the pliant and sibilant switch for our more noisy than unpleasant castigation. But there, persistent as are the roads old hunters made upon the hills of long ago, as are the ways our fathers went to market through glens for years untenanted, was the path we youngsters made between the highway and old Copenhagen's school!

Is it conceivable, I ask my old companions of that hillside seminary, that

Copenhagen should be dead? That a time should come when his thin, long, bent figure, carried on one of his own legs and one (as went our tradition) cut from an ash in the wood of Achnatra, should dart about the little school no more, and his tales of Nelson and the sea be all concluded?

He had been twenty years in the Navy, and had seen but a single engagement – the one that gave him his by-name, and cost him his leg. He came home with a pension, and settled in his native parish. He was elderly; he was – as we should think it now – ill-educated; he was without wife or child of his own; he had at times the habit of ran-dan, as we call a convivial rollicking. Heaven plainly meant him for a Highland school, and so he opened one – this same, so lowly to-day among the nettles. Of the various things he taught, the most I can remember (besides reading, which came, I fear, more by nature than by Copenhagen's teaching) was the geography of the Baltic, the graphic fact that Horatio Nelson nearly always wore a grey surtout, three ways of tying knots, and a song of epic character called "The Plains of Waterloo." What would perhaps be called a "special subject" nowadays was the art he taught us of keeping birds from cherry-trees. The cherry-trees grew up the front of Copenhagen's bachelor dwelling-house, half a mile from the school. When the fruit reddened, every scholar in the school (we numbered twelve or fourteen) rose at dawn for days and sat below the cherry-trees chanting a Gaelic incantation that never failed to keep away the predatory thrush. The odd thing was that Copenhagen, in spite of these precautions, never got a single cherry, and did not seem to care. We ate the cherries as they ripened, relieving each other alternately of the incantation; he came out to praise us for our industry, and never cast a glance aloft.

The fees for Copenhagen's college were uncertain – not only in payment, but in amount. When our parents asked him what was to pay for Bob or Sandy, the antique pensioner blew his nose with noisy demonstration, and invariably answered, "We don't know what we'll need till we see what we'll require." His requirements were manifestly few, for three-fourths of the pupils contributed nothing to the upkeep of the school but a diurnal peat in winter, and the others had their fees wholly expended on pens and paper for themselves when the flying stationer came round twice a year.

We grew to like and to respect old Copenhagen, knowing nothing of his ran-dans, that were confined to the town six miles away, and never were allowed to interfere with his duty to his pupils. He made no brilliant scholars, but he gave us a thousand pleasant, droll, and kindly memories that go far as a substitute for a superficial knowledge of Greek. I would myself have learned the cutlass from him, being the oldest of the pupils and the likeliest to make a good practitioner of that noble marine weapon; but, unhappily, I left the school and started my career in town the very day he had unearthed the sword and brought it forth for my first lesson.

It was there I learned that Copenhagen was the church precentor, and had his little vices, whereof our folks at home, with wisdom and delicacy, had never given us a hint. He used to come down to town each Sunday in a pair of tightly-strapped breeches, a black surtout, and what we called a three-storey hat. The preacher chose the psalm, but it was Copenhagen chose the tune. He had but half a dozen airs in all his repertory – Selma, Dundee, Martyrdom, Coleshill, and Dunfermline, and what he called "yon one of my own." I have sometimes been to the opera since; I fear, from knowledge gained by that experience, that the old man was not highly gifted for vocalism. Invariably he started on too high a key, and found that he had done so only when a bar or two was finished. With imperturbability unfailing, he just stopped short, and, leaning over his desk, said to the congregation, "We'll have another try at it, lads!" The service was an English one, but this touching confidence was in Gaelic, and addressed particularly to the men who, married or single, sat apart from the women.

While Copenhagen still led the praise to Coleshill and "yon one of his own," a pestilent innovator came to the place who knew music, and, unhappily, introduced a band of enterprising youths to the mysteries of harmony. He taught them bass and alto, and showed them how the melody of Dundee and Coleshill could be embellished and improved by those. The first Sunday these vocalists started to display their new art in the church, Copenhagen stopped in the middle of a verse to make a protest.

"I'll have none of your boom-boom singing here to put me all reel-rall," said he, "nor praising of the Lord with such theatricals," then baffled them by changing the air to "yon one of his own."

A bachelor by prejudice and conviction, he liked to hear of marriages, and when the "cries" were read he had for long – until a new incumbent made a protest – a cheerful, harmless habit of crying at the end of the announcement, "I have no objections to't whatever."

The new incumbent was less tolerant than his predecessor; to him was due the old man's retirement from the office of conductor of the psalmody. He would not countenance the ran-dans, nor consent to the perpetuation of Copenhagen's ancient manners in the precentor's desk. First of all he claimed the right of intimating the tunes as well as the psalms to be sung to them, and sought thereby to put an end to the unseemly "yon one of my own"; but Copenhagen started what air he pleased, no matter what was intimated, and more often than before it was his own creation. Then were thrust upon the old man wooden boards with the names of half a dozen psalm tunes printed on them. They were to be displayed in front of the desk as required, and thus save all necessity for any verbal intimation. But Copenhagen generally showed them upside down, and still maintained his vested rights to start what airs he chose. "I think we agreed on Martyrdom in the vestry," said the minister once, exasperated into a protest in front of the congregation when Copenhagen started "yon one." "So we did, so we

64

did – I mind fine; but I shifted my mind," said Copenhagen, looking up, and cleared his throat to start again. "Upon my word," said he to sympathisers in the afternoon, "upon my word the man's a fair torment!"

Old Copenhagen's most notable ran-dans were after he had demitted office as musician, out of patience at last with the "torment." They were such guileless, easily induced excesses, so marked by an incongruous propriety, that I hesitate to speak of them as more than innocent exhilarations. 'Twas then his surtout was most spick and span, his manner most urbane and engaging. The poorest gangrel who addressed him on the highway then was "sir" to Copenhagen, and a boy had but to look at him to be assured of a halfpenny. His timber leg went tapping over the causeways then with an illusive haste, for it was Copenhagen's wish to be thought a man immersed profoundly in affairs. He spoke in his finest English (reserved for moments of importance) of the Admiralty, and he never entered the inn without having in his hand a large packet of blue envelopes tied with a boot-lace, to suggest important and delicate negotiations with some messenger from the First Lord. Once, I remember, he came out of the inn with a suspicious-looking bulge in the tail-pocket of his surtout. As he passed the Beenickie and Jock Scott and me standing at the factor's corner, and punctiliously returned the naval salute he always looked for from his own old pupils, a "Glenorchy pint" (as it was called) fell out of his pocket in the street, without suffering any damage. He never paused a moment or looked round, and the Beenickie cried after him, "You have dropped something, Mr Bain." "It is just a trifle, lads," he answered without looking back; "I will get it when I return," and pursued his way to his house, six miles away. He was ashamed, I suppose, of the exposure.

Another time – on the night of St John's, when the local Freemasons had their flambeau march, and every boy who carried a torch got threepence on production of its stump the following day (which induced some to cut their stumps in two, and so get sixpence) – I saw old Copenhagen falling down an outside stair. I hastened to his assistance, suffering sincere alarm and pity for my ancient dominie. He was, luckily, little the worse. "I was coming down in any case, John," said he benignly. "Man! I am always vexed I never learned you the fencing with the cutlass, for you were a promising lad." "I am sorry too, Mr Bain," said I, though indeed I could not see that a clerk in a law office would find the accomplishment in question of much use to him. "I knew your Uncle Jamie," he added. "Him and me was pretty chief. You will say nothing about my bit of a glide, John: I was coming down at any rate, I assure you."

I should like my last reminiscence of old Copenhagen to be more reputable, for his own last words in gossiping of any one, no matter how foolish or vile, were always generous. And I recall a day when he came from his distant seminary through deep drifts of snow to the town to post a letter that he wished me to revise first. The 'Courier' of the week was full of tales of misery among our troops in the Crimean trenches, and Copenhagen's sympathies were fired. His letter was a suggestion to the Admiralty that in these times of stress it might help my Lords a little if they were relieved of the payment of the pension of Archibald Bain, late of H.M.S. *Elephant*. He was very old, and frail, and tremulous in these days; his hand of write would have sorely puzzled any one but me, who knew so well its eccentricities. His folly touched me to the core; I knew his object, but for the life of me I could not read his letter.

"I think it would be a mistake to send it, Mr Bain," I said, when he explained.

"Havers!" said he. "What I want you to tell me is if it is shipshape and Bristol fashion, eh? and not likely to give offence. Read it, man, read it!"

"Read it out to me yourself, Mr Bain," I stammered, "the thing's beyond me."

He put on his spectacles and looked closely at his own scrawl. "I declare to you," he said in a little, laughingly, "I declare to you I cannot read a word of her myself. But no matter, John, we'll just let her go as she stands; they're better scholars in London than what we are."

The letter went, but I never heard that the British Admiralty availed itself of an offer so unusual and kind.

I thought of these things yesterday as I passed the ruins of Copenhagen's school. How far, since then, have travelled the feet that trod there; how far, how weary, how humbled, how elate, how prosperous, how shamefully down at heel? Dear lads, dear girls, wherever you be, my old companions, were we not here in this poor place, among the hazel and the fern, most fortunate and happy? Has the wide world we travel through for fame or fortune – or, better still, content – added aught to us of joy we did not have (at least in memory) in those irrecoverable, enduring, summer days? Now it is mist for ever on the hill, and the rain-rot in the wood, and clouds and cares chasing each other across our heavens, and flowers that flame from bud to blossom and smoulder into dust almost before we have caught their perfume; then, old friends, we pricked our days out leisurely upon a golden calendar: the scent of the morning hay-fields seemed eternal.

The Silver Drum

I

FIFTY yards to the rear of the dwelling-house the studio half hid itself amongst young elms and laurel bushes, at its outside rather like a granary, internally like a chapel, the timbers of the roof exposed and umber-stained, with a sort of clerestory for the top light, a few casts of life-size statues in the corners, and two or three large bas-reliefs of Madonnas and the like by Donatello helping out the ecclesiastical illusion. It was the last place to associate with the sound of drums, and yet I sat for twenty minutes sometimes stunned, sometimes fascinated, by the uproar of asses' skin. The sculptor who played might, by one less unconventional, be looked upon as seriously sacrificing his dignity in a performance so incongruous with his age and situation. But I have always loved the whimsical; I am myself considered somewhat eccentric, and there is a *rapport* between artistic souls that permits – indeed, induces – some display of fantasy or folly when they get into each other's society apart from the intolerant folks who would think it lunacy for a man of over middle age to indulge in the contre-dance of "Petronella" at a harvest-home, or display any accomplishment with the Jew's-harp.

Urquhart, at the time when I sat to him, was a man of sixty years or thereabout; yet he marched up and down the floor of his workshop with the step of a hill-bred lad, his whole body sharing the rhythm of his beating, his clean-shaven face with the flush of a winter apple, the more noticeable in contrast with the linen smock he used as an overall while at work among his clay. The deep old-fashioned side-drum swinging at his groin seemed to have none of a drum's monotony. It expressed (at all events to me that have some fancy) innumerable ecstasies and emotions – alarms, entreaties, defiances, gaieties, and regrets, the dreadful sentiment of forlorn hopes, the murmur of dubious battalions in countries of ambush. The sound of the drum is, unhappily, beyond typographical expression, though long custom makes us complacently accept "rat-a-tat-tat" or "rub-a-dub-dub" as quite explanatory of its every phrase and accent; but I declare the sculptor brought from it the very pang of love. Alternated with the martial uproar of rouses, retreats, chamades, and marches that made the studio shake, it rose into the clerestory and lingered in the shades of the umber roof, this gentle combination of taps and *roulades,* like the appeal of one melodiously seeking admission at his mistress's door.

"You had no idea that I handled sticks so terrifically?" said he, relinquishing the instrument at last, and returning to his proper task of recording my lineaments in the preparatory clay.

"You play marvellously, Mr Urquhart," I said, astonished. "I had no idea you added the drum to your – to your accomplishments."

"Well, there you have me revealed – something of a compliment to you, I assure you, for I do not beat my drum for everybody. If I play well it is, after all, no wonder, for with a side-drum and a pair of sticks I earned a living for seven years and travelled among the most notable scenes of Europe."

"So?" I said, and waited. He pinched the clay carefully to make the presentment of the lobe of my ear, and stood back from his work a moment to study the effect.

"Yes," he said, "few people know of it; and perhaps it is as well, for it might not be counted wholly to the credit of an R.S.A. if it were known; but for seven years I played the side-drum in the ranks of the 71st. I played from Torres Vedras to the Pyrenees, at Vimiera, Corunna, Talavera, Busaco, Ciudad Rodrigo, Badajos, Quatre Bras, and Waterloo. Lord! the very names go dirling through my heart. They were happy days, I assure you, when I – when I –"

"Thumped the skin," I ventured foolishly, as he paused to make a line of some importance on my effigy.

He corrected me with a vexed air.

"Thumped, my dear sir, is scarcely the word I should use under the circumstances. That hackneyed verb of every dolt who has neither ear nor imagination should not be chosen by a fellow-artist, a man of letters, to describe the roll of the drum. My happiest days, as I was about to say, were when I carried Kildalton's silver drum, for which this one is but an indifferent substitute."

"Well, at least," said I lamely, "the drummer of the 71st has gone pretty far in another art than music."

"It is very good of you to say so," remarked Urquhart, with quiet dignity and an old-fashioned bow. "I trust, by-and-by, with assiduity to become as good a sculptor as I was a drummer."

"How did you happen to join the Army?" I asked, anxious to have him follow up so promising an introduction.

"Because I was a fool. Mind, I do not regret it, for I had at the same time, in my folly, such memorable and happy experiences as quite improperly (as you might think) never come to the doorstep of the very wise. Still, I joined the Army in a fool's escapade, resenting what seemed to me the insufferable restrictions of a Scottish manse. My father was incumbent of a parish, half Highland, half Lowland. At sixteen I came home from

Edinburgh and my first session of the University there; at sixteen and a half I mutinied against sixpence a week of pocket-money and the prospect of the Divinity Hall for one (as I felt) designed by Heaven for Art, and with a borrowed name and an excellently devised tale of orphan-hood, took a bounty in the territorial regiment. They put me to the drums. They professed to find me so well suited there that they kept me at them all the time I was a King's man, in spite of all my protests, and there, if you are in the mood for a story, I had an experience.

"The corps had two drums of silver, one of which was entrusted to me. They were called 'Kildalton's drums,' in compliment to their donor, from whose lands no fewer than four companies of the 71st had been embodied. They were handsome instruments, used only for stately occasions, and mine, at least, so much engaged my fancy that I liked to keep it shining like a mirror; and the cords and tassels of silk – pleated, as we were told, by Kildalton's daughter – appealed so much to the dandiacal in me, I fretted to have them wet on a parade. You can fancy, therefore, my distress when my darling was subjected to the rough work and hazards of the sack of Ciudad Rodrigo.

"Our corps on that occasion was in the Light Division. While Picton's men, away to our left and nearer the river, were to attack the great breach made in the ramparts by our guns on the Tessons, we were to rush into a lesser breach farther east. The night was black and cold to that degree I could not see the fortress at a hundred yards, and could scarcely close my fingers on the drum-sticks as I beat for the advance of Napier's storming party. The walls we threatened burst in tongues of flame and peals of thunder. Grape-shot tore through our three hundred as we crossed the ditch; but in a moment we were in the gap, the bayonets busy as it were among wine-skins, the footing slimy with blood, and a single drum (my comrade fell mortally wounded in the ditch) beat inside the walls for the column outside to follow us."

"Yes, yes," I said, impatient, for Urquhart drew back abstracted, checking his tale to survey the effect of his last touch upon my eyebrows.

He smiled.

"Why," said he, "I hardly thought it would interest you," and then went on deliberately.

"I need not tell you," he said, "how quick was our conquering of the French, once we had got through the walls. My drum was not done echoing back from Sierra de Francisca (as I think the name was), when the place was ours. And then – and then – there came the sack! Our men went mad. These were days when rapine and outrage were to be expected from all victorious troops; there might be some excuse for hatred of the Spaniard on the part of our men, whose comrades, wounded, had been left to starve at Talavera – but surely not for this. They gorged with wine, they swarmed in lawless squads through every street and alley; swept through every dwelling, robbing and burning; the night in a while was white with fires, and the town was horrible with shrieks and random musket-shots and drunken songs.

"Some time in the small hours of the morning, trying to find my own regiment, I came with my drum to the head of what was doubtless the most dreadful street that night in Europe. It was a lane rather than a street, unusually narrow, with dwellings on either side so high that it had some semblance to a mountain pass. At that hour, if you will credit me, it seemed the very gullet of the Pit: the far end of it in flames, the middle of it held by pillagers who fought each other for the plunder from the houses, while from it came the most astounding noises – oaths in English and Portuguese, threats, entreaties, and commands, the shrieks of women, the crackling of burning timber, occasionally the firing of weapons, and through it all, constant, sad beyond expression, a deep low murmur, intensely melancholy, made up of the wail of the sacked city.

"As I stood listening some one called out, 'Drummer!'

"I turned, to find there had just come up a general officer and his staff, with a picket of ten men. The General himself stepped forward at my salute and put his hand on my drum, that shone brightly in the light of the conflagrations.

"'What the deuce do you mean, sir,' said he with heat, 'by coming into action with my brother's drum? You know very well it is not for these occasions.'

"'The ordinary drums of the regiment were lost on Monday last, sir,' I said, 'when we were fording the Agueda through the broken ice.' And then, with a happy thought, I added, 'Kildalton's drums are none the worse for taking part in the siege of Ciudad Rodrigo. This was the first drum through the walls.'

"He looked shrewdly at me and gave a little smile. 'H'm,' he muttered, 'perhaps not, perhaps not, after all. My brother would have been pleased, if he had been alive, to know his drums were here this night. Where is the other one?'

"'The last I saw of it, sir,' I answered, 'was in the ditch, and Colin Archibald, corporal, lying on his stomach over it.'

"'Dead?'

"'Dead, I think, sir.'

"'H'm!' said the General. 'I hope my brother's drum's all right, at any rate.' He turned and cried up the picket. 'I want you, drummer,' he said, 'to go up that lane with this picket, playing the assembly. You understand? These devils fighting and firing there have already shot at three of my officers, and are seemingly out of their wits. We will give them a last chance. I don't deny there is danger in what I ask you to do, but it has to be done. The men in there are mostly of Pack's Portuguese and the dregs of our own corps. If they do not come out with you I shall send in a whole regiment to them and batter their brains out against the other end, if the place is, as I fancy, a *cul-de-sac*. March!'

"I went before the picket with my drum rattling and my heart in my mouth. The pillagers came round us jeering, others assailed us more seriously by throwing from upper windows anything they could conveniently lay hand on (assuming it was too large or too valueless to pocket), but we were little the worse till in a lamentable moment of passion one of the picket fired his musket at a window. A score of pieces flashed back in response, and five of our company fell, while we went at a double for the end of the lane.

"'By Heaven!' cried the sergeant when we reached it, 'here's a fine thing!' The General had been right – it was a *cul-de-sac!* There was nothing for us then but to return.

"You have never been in action; you cannot imagine," Urquhart went on, "the exasperating influence of one coward in a squad that is facing great danger. There were now, you must know, but six of us, hot and reckless with anger, and prepared for anything – all but one, and he was in the fear of death. As I went before the picket drumming the assembly and the sergeant now beside me, this fellow continually kicked my heels, he kept so close behind. I turned my head, and found that he marched crouching, obviously eager to have a better man than himself sheltering him from any approaching bullet.

"'You cowardly dog!' I cried, stepping aside, 'come out from behind me and die like a man!' I could take my oath the wretch was sobbing! It made me sick to hear him, but I was saved more thought of it by the rush of some women across the lane, shrieking as they ran, with half a company at least of Portuguese at their heels. With a shout we were after Pack's scoundrels, up a wide pend close (as we say in Scotland) that led into a courtyard, where we found the valorosas prepared to defend the position with pistol and sword. A whole battalion would have hesitated to attack such odds, and I will confess we swithered for a moment. A shot came from the dark end of the entry and tore through both ends of my drum.

"'We're wretched fools to be here at all,' said lily-liver, plainly whimpering, and at that I threw down my outraged instrument, snatched his musket from him, and charged up the close with the other four. The Portuguese ran like rabbits; for the time, at least, the women were safe, and I had a remorse for my beloved drum.

"I left the others to follow, hurried into the lane, and found the poltroon was gone, my drum apparently with him. Ciudad Rodrigo was darker now, for the fires were burning low. It was less noisy, too; and I heard halfway up the lane the sound of a single musket-shot. I ran between the tall tenements; the glint of bright metal filled me with hope and apprehension. A man lay in the gutter beside my drum, and a Portuguese marauder, who fled at my approach, stood over him with a knife.

"The man in the gutter was the General, with his brother's drum slung to him, and the sticks in his hands, as if he had been playing. He was unconscious, with a bullet through his shoulder."

II

Urquhart stopped his tale again, to wheel round the platform on which I sat, so as to get me more in profile.

"This looks marvellously like stuff for a story," I said to him as he set to work again upon the clay. "My professional interests are fully aroused. Please go on."

He smiled again.

"I am charmed to find you can be so easily entertained," said he. "After all, what is it? Merely a trifling incident. Every other man who went through the Peninsular campaign came on experiences, I am sure, far more curious. My little story would have ended in the lane of Ciudad Rodrigo had not three companies of the 71st – mainly invalids after Badajos – been sent to Scotland for a whiff of their native air, and the fascination of recruits. I had got a spent ball in the chest at Badajos. I, too, had that gay vacation. I went with my silver drum to the county it came from. It was glorious summer weather. For three weeks we were billeted in the county town; for a fortnight I would not have changed places with King George himself."

"Mr Urquhart," I said, "I have a premonition. Here comes in the essential lady."

The sculptor smiled.

"Here, indeed," he said, "comes in the lady. There are, I find, no surprises for a novelist. We were one day (to resume my story) in the burgh square, where a market was being held, and hopes were entertained by our captain that a few landward lads might nibble at the shilling. Over one side of the square towered a tall whitewashed house of many windows; and as I, with a uniform tunic that was the pride of the regimental tailor, five feet eleven, twenty-one years of age, and the vanity of a veteran, played my best to half a dozen fifes, I noticed the lady at a window – the only window in all that massive house-front to manifest any interest in our presence or performance. I turned my silver drum a little round upon my leg that it might reflect more dazzlingly the light of the afternoon sun, and threw into my beats and rolls the most graceful style that was at my command, all the while with an eye on madam. It was my youthful conceit that I had caught her fancy when, a little later – our sergeants busy among the rustics – she came out from the house and over where I sat apart beside my drum on the steps of the market cross. She was younger than myself, a figure so airy and graceful, you would swear that if she liked she could dance upon blue-bells without bruising a petal; she had hair the colour of winter bracken in sunshine, and the merriest smile.

"'Excuse me,' said she, 'but I *must* look at the darling drum – the sweet drum,' and caught the silken cords in her fingers, and ran a palm of the daintiest hand I had ever seen over the shining barrel.

"I thought she might, with more creditable human sentiment, have had less interest in my drum and more in me, but displayed my instrument with the best grace I could command.

"'Do you know why I am so interested?' she asked in a little, looking at me out of deep brown eyes in which I saw two little red-coated drummers, a thing which gave me back my vanity and made me answer her only with a smile. Her cheek for the first time reddened, and she hurried to explain. 'They are Kildalton's drums. Mr Fraser of Kildalton was my father, who is dead, and my mother is dead too; and I pleated and tied these cords and tassels first. How beautifully you keep them!'

"'Well, Miss Fraser,' said I, 'I assure you I could not keep them better if I tried; but, after this, I shall have a better reason than ever for keeping them at their best,' a soldier's speech she smiled at as she turned away. As she went into the tall white house again she paused on the threshold and looked back for a moment at me, smiling, and for the first time since I took the bounty I rued my bargain, and thought I was meant for something more dignified than drumming. From that hour I lived in the eyes of Kildalton's daughter Margory. Once a week we went fifing and drumming through the square. She was on these occasions never absent from her window; there was never a smile awanting for the smart young gentleman who beat the silver drum. A second and a third time she came into the square to speak to me. I made the most of my opportunities, and she was speedily made to discover in the humble drummer a fellow of race and education, a fellow with a touch of poetry, if you please. She was an orphan, as I have indicated – the ward of an uncle, a general, at the time abroad. She lived on the surviving fortune of Kildalton, in the tall white house, with an elderly aunt and a servant. At our third interview – we have a way of being urgent in the Army – she had trysted to meet me that evening in the wood behind the town.

"Let me do the girl justice, and say that the drum of Kildalton brought her there, and not the drummer. At least, she was at pains to tell me so, for I had mentioned to her, with some of the gift of poetry I have mentioned, how infinitely varied were the possibilities of an instrument she would never have a proper chance to judge of in the routine of a fife-and-drum parade.

"My billet was at the back of the town, on the verge of a wood, with the window of my room opening on a sort of hunting-path that went winding through the heart of what I have called a wood, but was in actual fact a forest of considerable dimensions. I went out by the window that evening with my drum, and walked, as had been arranged, about a mile among the trees till I came to a narrow glen that cleft the hills, a burn of shallow water from the peaty uplands bickering at the bottom of it. A half moon swung like a halbert over the heights that were edged by enormous fir-trees, and the wood was melancholy with the continuous call of owls. They were soon silenced, for I began to play the silver drum.

"I began with the reveille, though it was a properer hour for the tattoo, playing it lightly, so that while it silenced the hooting owls it did not affright the whole forest. She came through the trees timidly, clothed, as I remember, in a gown of green. She might have been the spirit of the pine-plantings; she might have been a dryad charmed from the swinging boughs. 'Margory! Margory!' I cried, my heart more noisy than my drum had been, and clasped her to my arms. 'Here's a poor drummer, my dear,' I said, 'and you a queen. If you do not love me you were less cruel to take this dirk and stab me to the heart than act the heartless coquette.'

"She faintly struggled. Her hair fell loose in a lock or two from under her hat, surged on her shoulder, and billowed about my lips. Her cheek was warm; her eyes threw back the challenge of the silver moon over the tops of pine.

"'For a young gentleman from a kirk manse, Master Drummer, you have considerable impertinence,' said she, panting in my arms.

"'My name, dear Margory, is George, as I have told you,' I whispered, and I kissed her.

"'George, dear George,' said she, 'have done with folly! Let me hear the drumming and go home.'

"I swung her father's drum again before me and gave, in cataracts of sound, or murmuring cascades, the sentiments of my heart.

"'Wonderful! Oh, wonderful!' she cried, entranced; so I played on.

"The moon went into a cloud; the glade of a sudden darkened; I ceased my playing, swung the drum again behind, and turned for Margory.

"She was gone!

"I cried her name as I ran through the forest, but truly she was gone."

Urquhart stopped his story and eagerly dashed some lines upon the clay. "Pardon!" he said. "Just like that, for a moment. Ah! that is something like it!"

"Well, well!" I cried. "And what followed?"

"I think – indeed, I know – she loved me, but – I went back to the war without a single word from her again."

"Oh, to the deuce with your story!" I cried at that, impatient. "I did not bargain for a tragedy."

"In truth it is something of a farce, as you shall discover in a moment," said the sculptor. "Next day the captain sent for me. 'Do you know General Fraser?' said he, looking at a letter he held in his hand. I told him I had not the honour. 'Well,' said he, 'it looks as if the family had a curious *penchant* for the drum, to judge from the fact that his brother gave yours to the regiment, and also' – here he smiled slyly – 'from the interest of his niece. He is not an hour returned from Spain to his native town when he asks me to send you with your drum to his house at noon.'

"'Very good, sir,' I answered, with my heart thundering, and went out of the room most hugely puzzled.

"I went at noon to the tall white house, and was shown into a room where sat Margory, white to the lips, beside the window, out of which she looked after a single hopeless glance at me. A middle-aged gentleman in mufti, with an empty sleeve, stood beside her, and closely scrutinised myself and my instrument as I entered.

"'This is the – the person you have referred to?' he asked her, and she answered with a sob and an inclination of her head.

"'You have come – you are reputed to have come of a respectable family,' he said then, addressing me; 'you have studied at Edinburgh; you have, I am told, some pretensions to being something of a gentleman.'

"'I hope they are no pretensions, sir,' I answered warmly. 'My people are as well known and as reputable as any in Argyll, though I should be foolishly beating a drum.'

"'Very good,' said he, in no way losing his composure.

'I can depend on getting the truth from you, I suppose? You were with the 71st as drummer at Ciudad Rodrigo?'

"'I was, sir,' I replied. 'Also at Badajos, at Talavera, Busaco – '

"'An excellent record!' he interrupted. 'I might have learned all about it later had not my wound kept me two months in hospital after Ciudad. By the way, you remember being sent as drummer with a picket of men down a lane?'

"I started, gave a careful look at him, and recognised the General whose life I had doubtless saved from the pillaging Portuguese.

"'I do, sir,' I answered. 'It was you yourself who sent me.'

"He turned with a little air of triumph to Margory. 'I told you so, my dear,' said he. 'I got but a distant glimpse of him this forenoon, and thought I could not be mistaken.' And Margory sobbed.

"'My lad,' he said, visibly restraining some emotion, 'I could ask your drum-major to take the cords of Kildalton my brother's drum and whip you out of a gallant corps. I sent you with a picket – a brave lad, as I thought any fellow should be who played Kildalton's drum, and you came back a snivelling poltroon. Nay – nay!' he cried, lifting up his hand and checking my attempt at an explanation. 'You came out of that infernal lane whim-pering like a child, after basely deserting your comrades of the picket, and made the mutilated condition of your drum the excuse for refusing my order to go back again, and I, like a fool, lost a limb in showing you how to do your duty.'

"'But, General –' I cried out.

"'Be off with you!' he cried. 'Another word, and I shall have you thrashed at the triangle.'

"He fairly thrust me from the room, and the last I heard was Margory's sobbing.

"Next day I was packed off to the regimental depot, and some weeks later played a common drum at Salamanca."

The sculptor rubbed the clay from his hands and took off his overall.

"That will do to-day, I think," said he. "I am much better pleased than I was yesterday," and he looked at his work with satisfaction.

"But the story, my dear Mr Urquhart. You positively must give me its conclusion!" I demanded.

"Why in the world should that not be its conclusion?" said he, drawing a wet sheet over the bust. "Would you insist on the hackneyed happy ending?"

"I am certain you did not take your quittance from the General in that way. Your surely wrote to Margory or to him with an explanation?"

The sculptor smiled.

"Wrote!" cried he. "Do you think that so obvious an idea would not occur to me? But reflect again, I pray you, on the circumstances, – an obscure and degraded drummer – the daughter of one of the oldest families in the Highlands – the damning circumstantiality of her uncle's evidence of my alleged poltroonery. My explanation was too incredible for pen and paper; and the poltroon himself, the man who had brought the disgrace upon me, was beyond my identification, even had I known where to look for him."

"And yet, Mr Urquhart," I insisted, all my instincts as romancer assuring me of some other conclusion to a tale that had opened on a note so cheerful, "I feel sure it was neither a tragedy nor a farce in the long-run."

"Well, you are right," he confessed, smiling. "It was my drum that lost me the lady before ever I met her, as it were, and it was but fair that my drum should be the means of my recovering her ten years later. A reshuffling of the cards of fortune in my family brought me into a position where I was free to adopt the career of Art, and by-and-by I had a studio of my own in Edinburgh. It was the day of the portrait bust in marble. To have one's own effigy in white, paid for by one's own self, in one's own hall, was, in a way, the fad of fashionable Edinburgh. It was profitable for the artist, I admit, but – but –"

"But it palled," I suggested.

"Beyond belief! I grew to hate the appearance of every fresh client, and it was then that I sought the solace of this drum. When a sitter had gone for the day I drummed the vexation out of me, feeling that without some such relief I could never recover a respect for myself. And by-and-by I began to discover in the instrument something more than a relief for my feelings of revolt against the commercial demands on my art. I found in it an inspiration to rare emotions: I found in it memory. I found, in the reveilles and chamades that I played in fields of war and in the forest to my Margory, love revived and mingled with a sweet regret, and from these – memory, regret, and love – I fashioned what have been my most successful sculptures.

"One day a gentleman came with a commission for his own portrait. It was General Fraser! Of course, he did not recognise me. Was it likely he should guess that the popular sculptor and the lad he had sent in disgrace from the tall white house in the distant Highland burgh town were one? Nor did I at first reveal myself. Perhaps, indeed, he would never have discovered my identity had not his eyes fallen on my drum.

"'You have had a military subject lately?' he said, indicating the instrument.

"'No, General,' I answered on an impulse. 'That is a relic of some years of youthful folly when I played Kildalton's silver drum, and it serves to solace my bachelor solitude.'

"'Heavens!' he cried; 'you, then, are the drummer of Ciudad Rodrigo?'

"'The same,' I answered, not without a bitterness. 'But a very different man from the one you imagine.' And then I told my story. He listened in a curious mingling of apparent shame, regret, and pleasure, and when I had ended was almost piteous in his plea for pardon. 'The cursed thing is,' he said, 'that Margory maintains your innocence till this very day.'

"'That she should have that confidence in me,' said I, 'is something of a compensation for the past ten years. I trust Miss Margory – I trust your niece is well.'

"The General pondered for a moment, then made a proposition.

"'I think, Mr Urquhart,' said he, 'that a half-winged old man is but a poor subject for any sculptor's chisel, and, with your kind permission, I should prefer to have a portrait of Miss Margory, whom I can swear you will find quite worthy of your genius.'

"And so," said Urquhart in conclusion, "and so, indeed, she was."

"There is but one *dénouement* possible," I said with profound conviction, and, as I said it, a bar of song rose in the garden, serene and clear and unexpected like the first morning carol of a bird in birchen shaws. Then the door of the studio flung open, and the singer entered, with the melody checked on her lips whenever she saw the unexpected stranger. She had hair the colour of winter bracken in sunshine, and the merriest smile.

"My daughter Margory," said the sculptor. "Tell your mother," he added, "that I bring our friend to luncheon."

The Scottish Pompadour

SEVERAL years ago there was no figure more conspicuous on the boulevards of Paris at the fashionable hour than that of the dandy called le Pompadour écossais by the journals. He had what will command attention anywhere, but most of all in Paris – the mould of an Apollo, a tailor of genius, the money of a Monte Cristo, and above all, Mystery. In the speech of this tall, dark, and sober-visaged exquisite there was no hint of a foreign nationality. His French was perfect; his idioms were correctly chosen; only his title, Lord Balgowie, and a foible for the use of the checkered stuff his countrymen call tartan, in his waistcoats, proclaimed that he was a Scot. That he should elect to spend his time in Paris seemed but natural to the boulevardiers: it is the only place for young gentlemen of spirit and the essential cash; but why should he feed himself like an anchorite while he surfeited his friends? why, with such a gay exterior, should be allied a mind so sober, private character so blameless and austere? These problems exercised the speculations of the café tables all the summer.

In the rue Adolphe Yvon, one of the most exclusive and expensive streets in Paris, near enough to the Bois de Boulogne to be convenient for morning exercise, but far enough removed to be without the surge and roar of the tides of life that beat there in the afternoons, the Pompadour écossais had a mansion like a palace, where he entertained the fashionable world with the aid of a cook who seemed possessed of magic powers to startle and delight, a wine-cellar incredibly comprehensive, and a retinue of servants such as the President of the Republic himself could not command. If he dined at his house alone, he dined with all the grandiose formality of Lucullus; if he patronised a restaurant, he must have his private cabinet and a menu unbelievingly extravagant. But strictly speaking, he never dined alone, either in the rue Adolphe Yvon, Voisin's, or Paillard's: he was invariably accompanied by a fellow-countryman, who was his secretary or companion – a fellow saturnine and cynical, who ate and drank voraciously, while his master was content with the simplest viands and a glass of water.

They had come in spring to the *Ville Lumière*, and stepped, as it were, from the wagon-lit of the P.L.M. train from the South into the very vortex of frivolity. You saw the Pompadour écossais in the morning riding in the Bois on a snowy Irish hunter, wearing garments of a tone and cut that promptly set the fashion to the gommeaux, with a boutonnière of orchids;

driving his coach through the avenues of Versailles in the afternoon with a coat of gendarme blue with golden buttons; at the clubs, the galleries, the opera, the cafés, the coulisses of the theatre – always the very latest cry in fashion, ever splendid and inscrutable! Withal, he never had so much as a sou in his pocket to buy a newspaper; his secretary paid for all, and paid with nothing less than gold. Balgowie, arbiter of elegance, envied by young men for his style, was adored by the most fastidious and discerning women for his sensibility, which was curiously out of keeping with his life of waste.

Quite as deeply interested in the Pompadour as any of the butterflies who fluttered round him in the rue Adolphe Yvon was a poor old widow, wholly unknown, in Scotland, for every Saturday she had a letter from her son, Balgowie's secretary. She read of childish escapades, inordinate and unwholesome pleasures, reckless prodigality.

"What a miserable life!" she would exclaim at the news of some fresh imbecility, as it seemed to her. "A hundred pounds for a breakfast! Five hundred pounds for a picture to a lady! Oh, Jamie, Jamie, what a master!"

She grieved, indeed, exceedingly about the sinful course of life in which her son was implicated, and more than once, for his soul's sake, asked him to come back to Scotland, but always he temporised. With Lord Balgowie he enjoyed a comfortable salary; he had no profession at his hands, although he had had the best of educations, thanks to his parents' self-denial, and he saw himself doomed for a term of years to follow the progress of his rakish patron.

Her only comfort was in the shrewd and sober nature of his comments on his master's follies. "I have looked at his manner of life in all ways, mother," he wrote, "and it seems to me deplorable. Once I had the notion to be wealthy for the sake of the independence and the power for good that money can command; now I can see it has a cankering influence on the soul. I have gone with my lord to every part of Europe, looking for content and – in his own state – simple honesty, for friends to trust, and a creditable occupation for the mind. Nothing in all the capitals among the rich but idleness and riot and display, cunning intrigue, self-seeking, and calculation. Thank God that you're poor!"

Not so very poor, though, for he sent her thirty shillings every week, a benefaction that enabled her to share among the really poor who were her neighbours. For years that sum had come to her with his letters every Saturday, often from towns whose names in their foreign spelling were unknown to her; a sense of opulence that caused her some uneasiness had more than once compelled her to protest. "I am sure you deprive yourself," she wrote, "and half that money would do me finely. You should be saving, laddie; some day you will want to marry."

"Marry," he wrote her back, incontinent; "I am here in a world of mannequins, and have yet to see the woman I could be happy to sit with in auld age by a Scottish fire."

But he was not always to be of that mind. One day her weekly letter held the fabulous sum of twenty pounds, and a hint of his infatuation for a lady he had met in Paris. His mother read his rhapsodies about the lass; they were, she noticed, more about her wit and beauty than about her heart. And in his letter was an unfamiliar undertone of apprehension, secrecy, evasion, which her mother sense discerned.

.   .   .

The Pompadour écossais rose one morning from his bed, which once belonged to Louis Quatorze, in the rue Adolphe Yvon; broke his fast on a bowl of coffee and a roll, and having dressed himself, as he always did, without a valet, with as much fastidiousness as if he were the Duke de Morny, rode for an hour in the wood, and later drove his English coach, with his English horses, English grooms, and English post-horn, out to the garden of St Germain. He was unusually resplendent, from his hat of silk, broad-brimmed, widely banded with bombazine, to high-heeled military shoes which seemed moulded to his feet, and had never known an unguent, but were polished daily to a fine dull lustre by the shin-bone of a deer. Upon his coat lapel was a green carnation that had cost a louis; his secretary sat behind him on the box, a man of undistinguished presence, wearing a sardonic smile; on the seats behind him was a company of guests for whom the lord had sieved the most exclusive salons of the capital – Prevost and Chatran, Chelmonski the Napoleonic painter, Paul Delourade the poet, half a dozen women of the most impeccable repute, and among them Mathilde de Langan with her ponderous mother, who was overjoyed to think that, after years of fruitless strategy, she was like to find an eminently eligible son-in-law in Lord Balgowie.

The girl was altogether lovely, exquisitely moulded, in the delicious gush of health and youthfulness, a miracle of grace with an aspect that recalled the pictures of Italian Madonnas; a brow benign and calm, a little tender mouth designed rather for prayer than for kissing, eyes purple black, profound as wells and prone to an alluring pensiveness.

They reached St Germain; stabled the horses, lunched upon the terrace that looks widely over the plain of Paris; obsequious silent servants hung about the tables; food and banter, wine and laughter, fruit and flowers engaged the company as it sat between the parterres, under awnings; and apart a little, looking on with eyes that gleamed at times with furtive and malicious entertainment, sat the secretary.

"That is a singular man of yours, milord," remarked Mathilde, who sat beside the Pompadour. "I have never seen him smile but in derision."

"He is a man with a peculiar sense of humour," said the Pompadour, regarding her with gravely tender eyes. "I should not be surprised if the whole interior of that apparently saturnine body is at this moment rumbling with laughter."

"Vraiment? What should he be laughing at?" asked the lady, whose judicious mother with discreet consideration sought a wicker arm-chair, screened herself with a quite unnecessary sunshade, and prepared to nap.

"At what he must think the folly of – of my quest for pleasure. He is, you know, my countryman, and the happy-starred among us find content and joy in the very cheapest, simplest entertainment. The cost of – of those flowers alone, perhaps he calculates at this moment, would suffice to keep his mother a fortnight."

"Mon Dieu! has he got a mother?" said the lady airily. "To look at that rugged form and the square hard countenance, I would have thought he had been chipped from granite. But I hope the dear mother is not really hungry. Do you know her?"

"I am privileged to read her letters once a week," said the Pompadour.

"That must be most amusing."

"It is at least instructive; she has her own ideas of the life of fashion, and the character of le Pompadour."

"Does she laugh, too, internally?"

"I fancy not," said the Pompadour reflectively; "I think it is more likely that she prays."

"How droll!" said the saintly lips. "But I suppose it is the best that one can do when one is poor. If I were so rich as you, and derived so much edification from her epistles, I should give her money."

"More than she has from her son, who loves her, would make her miserable. Sixty years of strict frugality spoil the constitution for excess, and two guineas a week would make her as uncomfortable as one of Joseph's dinners would."

"You, at least, do not show appreciation of your Joseph's dinners; you seem content with meagre soup and dry biscuits; one might think you were a physician, and we the subjects of experiment in indigestion."

Madame de Langan slept assuredly; the egrets on her hat bobbed most grotesquely; now and then she gurgled. The company had scattered, some to see the old home of the exiled James of England, some to walk on the forest fringes.

"Mathilde," said the Pompadour in a whisper, taking her hand in his and bending towards her with a look of burning concentration. "If I – if I were poor, could you love me?"

She started, bit her lip at a certain gaucherie in the question, but did not withdraw her hand. "I – I cannot say," she stammered; "isn't that a point for the little mother?" and she glanced at the sunshade hiding the ponderous sleeper.

"I know! I know! I know!" said the Pompadour in a fury of impatience. "But this is our Scottish fashion; first I must know from you, and then I shall consult your mother. Meanwhile, do you love me?"

"I have had no experience," said the lady, not much embarrassed. "You

81

have not told me yet if you love *me*, which is, I understand, the customary ritual."

"Mon Dieu!" said he in an excess of fervour, "I'm in a flame of passion and worship of you," and he crushed unconsciously her fingers in his two strong hands.

She winced. *"Oh, ce n'est pas gentil,"* she exclaimed, pulling away her hand. "You hurt me horribly." Then she smiled up in his face, provocatively coquettish, whispering, "To-morrow," for the other guests came trooping back upon the terrace.

On the following evening, when the dark was falling upon Paris, and the lamps began to bloom along the boulevards like flowers of fire, a little woman, simple, elderly, and timid, drove to the door of the mansion in the rue Adolphe Yvon, and asked to see his lordship's secretary.

"He is from home, madam," said the English servant, looking with curiosity at the homely figure.

"From home!" she exclaimed, beset with fears, and realising now more poignantly than ever all the hazards of her scheme. "I must see him to-night; I am his mother."

"He is meantime with his lordship at the restaurant of Voisin," said the domestic kindly. "Will you come in and wait for him?"

"Thank you, thank you!" she exclaimed; "but, if it were possible, I should like to see him now."

He put her in a cab, and gave the name of Voisin to the driver.

Voisin's, in the rue Cambon, is a quiet and unpretentious restaurant, dear to aristocratic Paris, since it looks so cheap and really is expensive. So quiet, so discreet, so restrained externally, men from the rural parts have been known to go boldly in, misapprehending, and before they had recovered from the blinding radiance of its tables, ask for a brioche and a mug of beer.

To-night it had, more speciously than usual, the aspect of a simple village inn: a hush prevailed; its waiters moved about on list, and spoke in whispers; le Pompadour écossais dined *en prince* upstairs with a merry company, in a chamber upon which the whole attention of the house was concentrated, from M. le Gérant down to the meanest kitchen scullion, for the evening's entertainment was upon a scale of reckless cost. Nothing would satisfy this wonderful man to-night but curious foods far-borne from foreign lands, strange rare beverages, golden vessels that had only once or twice been used in the Tuileries in the last days of the Empire. If diamonds could be crushed and turned by some miracle of alchemy into a palatable bouillon, he, or properly his secretary, would have cheerfully paid the cost. In an alcove screened by palms a string quartette played the most sensuous music, so exquisitely modulated that it seemed deliberately designed to harmonise with rallies of wit and peals of laughter.

Mathilde, who sat to the right of the host, and by her saintly aspect seemed at times incongruous with that company of fashion's fools, was for once silent, thoughtful, and demure.

"You have not told me yet if I may hope," said the Pompadour to her in a tender undertone, "and we disperse in less than twenty minutes."

"Hush!" she interrupted, with an impetuous jewelled hand upon his knee; "your friend has his eye on us! That man makes me afraid – he looks so cold, so supercilious! I hate to have a man regard me so who is convulsed with inside laughter, as you say; he looks – more like a conscience than a human secretary!"

Le Pompadour cast a glance across the room to the chair from which his secretary was at the moment summoned by a whispered message from the manager of the restaurant.

"He is a student of life and men," said he. "It is his humour to put the follies of fashion underneath the microscope of a mind as searchingly analytical as a lens."

"I'm glad all Scots are not like that," said the lady fervently. "Now, you have the real French temperament, and the means to entertain it; your secretary, were he as rich as you, I'm sure would be a skinflint."

"There, I can swear, you misjudge him," said the Pompadour, – "a man born unhappy, and spoiled for any useful purpose, I am sorry for him."

"Get rid of him – get rid of him!" said the lady, with a cleverly simulated shudder.

"What!" said the Pompadour, regarding her with surprise, seeing for the first time cruelty in the mild Madonna eyes. "Upon the secretary's stipend there depend, you know, the comforts of a poor old Scottish lady –"

"There are so many openings for a perambulating conscience! Those canaille! I am sure his frigid countenance spoils your appetite; it would spoil mine – and you eat like a Trappist monk. Is that Scots too?"

"Gluttony is the one aristocratic vice to which I could never become accustomed," he replied. "I was – I was once, as many here to-night would think, quite poor!"

She started slightly, looked incredulous. "How provoking it must have been!" she said.

"No," he reflected soberly. "Happiness – to speak platitude – has wonderfully little to do with a bank account. You look so good and wise I thought you had discovered that."

She answered with deliberate acidity –

"I quite disagree. I, at all events, could never contemplate poverty with equanimity."

"Not poverty," he protested eagerly – "not poverty! The young, the earnest, and the hopeful know no poverty; they are not poor – where there is love," and he searched her eyes as if his very life depended on discovering there a sign of her agreement with his sentiment.

She glanced about her at the indications of the speaker's wealth and prodigality, smiled cynically, tapped him with her fan. "*Farceur!*" said she, "now you are romantic, and to talk romance in seriousness is ridiculous."

Of a sudden he saw her what she really was – vain, cruel, calculating, parched in soul, despite her saintly face. He stared at her, almost stunned by disillusion, seeing the corruption of her nature rise like a scum upon the purple eyes.

To the left of his chair the door of the reception salon opened at the moment, and a voice beyond it plucked him from the depths of his despondency. He rose, incredulous, and rushed into the room, where a little old woman, simple and abashed at her surroundings, stood beside the secretary.

"Mother!" he exclaimed, with his arms around her, almost doubtful of her actual presence. "I thought it was your wraith."

"I fear I come at an awkward time," she said pathetically; "but all alone in this strange city, what was I to do?"

"You come at the very time I want you," he replied. "I had – I had forgotten things. I have been play-acting, and the play is done! Was this" – and he turned to the pseudo-secretary – "was this a part of your entertainment, Lord Balgowie?"

"It is a most effective curtain," said the other, smiling kindly on the little woman; "but it was not, strictly speaking, in the manuscript. I am glad the play, as you say, is over; for I had begun to think you took the part, in one respect, too seriously. I am honoured to meet you, madam; you must be wearied after such a journey. Both of you go at once to the rue Adolphe Yvon, and I shall make the requisite apologies to the company."

He saw them to the street, and returned to join the guests. "Ladies and gentlemen," he said, with a manner they had never seen in him before, "Le Pompadour has taken his leave *à l'anglais*, and my little joke has terminated in the most dramatic fashion. I have long had a desire to see, as a spectator, what for a dozen years I was under the absurd impression was a life of pleasure; and, at the cost of paying the bills myself and lending my worthy young compatriot my name for a few months, I have had the most delicious and instructive entertainment. In many respects he filled the part of Lord Balgowie better than ever I could do; but two things rather spoiled his admirable presentation – a homely taste in viands, and his honest heart!"

The Tale of the
Boon Companion

"EVERY man his boon companion, every man his maid," they say in Argyll. Somewhere in the wide world are both the man and the maid, but not always do they come to your door. You may pass the maid at the market, never thinking she was meant to mother your bairns, and her lot thereafter may be over many hills, baking bannocks of oaten meal on another man's hearth – that's your ill fortune; the boon companion may wander by the change-house where you sit drinking late – drinking late and waiting to learn the very songs he knows, and he may never come that road again; but whether that is good for you or ill is the most cunning of God's secrets. I could tell nine hundred tales and nine of boon companions who met the friend they were meant for, but I have still to learn the art of seeing the end from the beginning of any comradeship.

This particular and ancient history that I am telling is a story that is to be heard on winter nights in the fir-wood bothies of Upper Loch Finne. It is the story of an affair that happened in the wild year before the beginning of the little wars of Lorn.

Colkitto Macdonald and his Irishry and the Athol clans came, as the world knows, to Argyll, and carried the flambeau and the sword through every glen in the countryside. Into our peaceable neighbourhood, so harmless, so thriving and content, they marched on a winter's end – wild bearded fellows, ravenous at the eyes, lean as starved roebucks, cruel as the Badenoch wolves. They put mother and child to the pike; the best men of all our Gaelic people found the hero's death when standing up against these caterans, but uselessly. Carnus, Cladich, and Knapdale are thick with green spots where Clan Diarmaid's massacred people fell in the troubles.

To that rich and beautiful country the spring of the year comes always with vigour for the young heart. One feels the fumes of myrtle and fir in the head like a strong wine. It is the season of longing and exploits, and, if adventure is not in the way, the healthy young blood will be stirred to love or manly comradeship. Then the eye is keenest for the right girl, or (it may happen) the boon companion comes by the right chance, and leads the one waiting for him into the highroads where magic is at every corner, and old care is a carle to snap a finger at. There are no meats so sappy, no drink so generous and hearty, no sleep so sound as in that age and time.

It was in that season that the two men of my story met at a *ceilidh*, as we call a night gossiping, in a tacksman's house in Maam.

There had been singing of the true Gaelic songs and telling of Gaelic stories. A fellow, Alan, sat in a dusky corner of the room with a girl, Ealasaid, and they had little heed of song or story, but whispered the sweet foolishnesses of their kind in a world of their own, till a man new over from Cowal – Red John, by the by-name – stood to his feet and sang a Carrick ditty.

"I never heard better," said Alan in the girl's ear, for the new man and his new song had cried them back to the company.

"Good enough, I'm not denying," said she, "but he looks slack; you never saw a man with a low lip so full and a laugh so round and ready who was not given to wandering."

"Where from?" asked young Alan, his eyes roving between the girl and the man singing.

"From – oh! from good guidance," said she, flushing; "from the plain ways of his more common and orderly neighbours – from the day's work."

"The day's work," said Alan, "had no great hold on my fancy, and still and on I'm not what one would call lazy. I wish, do you know, I could sing yon jovial gentleman's songs, and think life so humoursome as I'll warrant a man with that laugh finds it."

He learned Red John's best songs before summer-time, for Red John was his boon companion.

They wandered, the pair of them, day after day and dusk after dusk, in the way of good-fellowship, coming on many jovial adventures, gathering curious songs, meeting free-handed folk and bits of good fortune. They went many a time on the carouse of true comradery, and Alan, who should be loving a girl, sat with this merry Cowal man in wayside ale-houses, drinking starlight and the drug of the easy heart from earthen jars.

"Could you come to meet me to-morrow?" once asked Ealasaid, finding her lover alone on his way to a new folly. She put a hand on his arm and leaned up against his side.

"Where would we go?" he asked, tucking a loose lock of her hair behind her ear, less for his love of trimness than to get some occupation for his eyes.

"It used to be enough that it was with me when I asked before," said Ealasaid, staying his fingers; "but my cousin-german in Coillebhraid asks us up to curds and cream."

"John and I are promised at a wrestling in the town," he said; "would the next day –"

The girl drew her screen about her like one smitten by a cold wind.

"Alan, Alan! your worst friend!" said she.

"The decentest lad in the world; he quarrels with none."

"For cowardice."

"He understands me in every key."

"So much the readier can he make you the fool."

"He has taught me the finest songs."

"To sing in the ale-house – a poor schooling, my dear!"

"I never before saw the jollity of living."

"It's no flattery to one Ealasaid; has he said aught of the seriousness of death?"

Alan hummed the end of a verse and then laughed slyly.

"Lass," said he, "does it make much differ that he thinks you the handsomest girl in the parish?"

"I would sooner you yourself thought me the plainest, and yet had some pleasure in my company."

"Yesterday (on a glass), he said your eyes were the fullest, your hair the yellowest, your step the lightest, your face the sweetest in all real Argyll."

"Then he's the man who should be doing your courting," said the girl, with a bitterness; and she went home sore-hearted.

The days passed on birds' feathers; the brackens coarsened in the gloomy places of the forest; the young of bird and beast lost themselves in the tangled richness of the field and wood. No rains came for many days, and the sun, a gallant horseman, rode from hill to hill, feasting his eye on the glens he saw too seldom.

In those hours the winds dozed upon the slimmest stem of heather; the burns, that for ordinary tear down our braes, bragging loud to the lip, hung back in friendly hollows under saugh-branch, rowan, and darach leaf; "but a little sleep," said they – "a little sleep, that we may finish a dream we woke in the middle of," and the grasshopper's chirrup drowned their prayer.

In their old fashion the glensfolk shifted for the time their homes to the shielings high up on the hills, in the breasts of the corries where are sappy levels that the heifers come to from the cropped glens like misers to a gentleman's table. While their cattle on the long day ends tugged the crisp grasses, the people would come out of their bothies and huts and sit in a company, above them the openings between the hills, the silver dusk that never grew dark, and the prickle of stars. Then Red John carried himself among the company like a chief, full of *bardachd*, of wit, of the most fairy music, so that even the girl whose lover he borrowed gave him credit for a warlock's charm.

It was not the genius of him, but the affable conduct and his gentleman's parts. A scamp, with duty near tugging at the cuff of his doublet, he went dancing through life, regardless as a bird. Had you a grievance against him? – he forgave you with a laugh, and took you by the elbow, telling some gaiety in your ear. Your most sober mood fell before his rallying like mist from the hillside in sun and breeze. Honest, true to his word as to his friend, fond of a glass, fond of a lass: they called him the boon friend of the shielings.

And wherever he went, this light-head, in humour and carelessness, Alan walked faithful at his heels, nearer his heart than any foster-brother, more and more learning his ways of idleness and diversion.

Ealasaid at last went to this Cowal fellow once complaining, with some shame, for a Highland girl has small heed to speak of the heart's business to any man but one.

"I'm sorry, my dear, I'm sorry," he said, with no pretence in the vexation of his brow. "I tempt no one to folly, and surely I'm not to blame for friendship to a lad so fine a woman can have the heart to think the best of."

"You are his blackest foe," she said stormily.

"I'm foe to none, woman," he cried, "except perhaps to a man they call Red John, and the worst enemy ever I had was welcome to share the last penny in my sporran. I have my weakness, I'll allow, but my worst is that my promise is better than my performance, and my most ill-judged acts are well intended."

"Blame yourself," said Ealasaid.

"I blame nobody," said he, laughing. "If other folk get such contentment out of their good deeds as I get out of my good intentions, it's no bad world to spend a while in."

"You're like the weak man in the *ceilidh* story," pressed the girl.

"How?" quo' he.

"Because you botch life," said she. "Let a girl tell it you. And the pity of it is you'll do it to the end."

At the worst of Ealasaid's heart-break and the folly of Alan and his boon companion, the men of Antrim and Athol came scouring over from Lorn into the glens of MacCailein Mor. They found a country far from ready to meet them, the leader himself from home, the sentinels sleeping, the forts without tenants. It was a bitter winter, and those gentlemen of Antrim and Athol kept their hides warm by chasing new-made orphans on to the frozen rivers. When the bairns ran on the ice crying, and went through it to a cold death, the good gentry laughed at the merriment of the spectacle. Down Aora glen went the bulk of them, and round the Gearran road to Shira glen, behind them smoking thatch and plundered folds.

Death struck with an iron hand at the doors of Maam, Elrigmore and Elrigbeg, Kilblane and Stuckgoy, and at Stuckgoy lived the girl of my story. She would have been butchered like her two brothers, by the fringe of Athol's army, but for her lover and his friend, who came when the need was the sorest for them, and led her out behind the spoiled township in the smoke of the burning byres.

There had been a break in the frost. It was a day of rain and mist, so the men who chased them lost them early.

"If we can reach the head of the glen first," said Alan, "there's safety in the Ben Bhuidhe cave." So the cave they ran for.

The cave is more on Ben Shean than Ben Bhuidhe, for all its name; a cunning hiding-place on the face of Sgornoch-mor rock, hanging over the deer wallows where the waters of Shira and Stacan sunder, seeking Lochow and Loch Finne. It was the home of the reiver when reiving was in vogue, a hold snug and easy for sleep, and deep enough for plunder. Fires might flash at night far ben in the heart of it, or songs might shake its roof, but never the wiser was the world out-by.

The way to the cave was off Shira side at the head of the glen, among whin bush and hazel, bending to the left over the elbow of Tomgorm, and a haw-tree hung above the face of Sgornoch-mor. The cave itself lay half-way down the rock, among a cluster of wild berry-bushes that clung finger and claw to a ledge so narrow that a man with a dirk could keep it against a score of clans. To reach it there was but one way all Glenshira folk knew, and none beside them – by a knotted rope that always lay at the root of the haw-tree for that purpose. Once in, and the rope with you, and your way to the foot of the rock was easy; but once in, and the rope awanting, and the place was your grave, for you might starve in the face of the birds that flapped on black feathers to their nests that were lower still on the rock.

The girl and her friends reached the head of the glen well before the band that followed them on the beaten road. There the mist fell off, and the bare hills closed in on a gullet the wind belched through. Before them was Tomgorm, and they took to the left and the climbing, Ealasaid and Alan in front and Red John behind them, checking the whistling of pibrochs at his lips.

"Poor girl, poor girl!" said he to himself, "I was wrong to have come between you in the long summer day, for here's in truth the black winter and the short day, homelessness and hunger, and the foe on our heels."

They got on the front of Sgornoch-mor, and all the north Highlands free of mist were in broken peaks before them, cut with glens, full of roads to liberty and safety, but too far off for a quarry before the hounds.

At the foot of the haw-tree was the rope in coils.

"There's little time to waste," said Red John, "for though I said nothing of it at the braefoot, I heard a corps of our followers too close on our heels for comfort. It would be leading them to our den below, and us to some trouble, if they saw the way we went. Will you go first, mistress, and Alan and I will follow?"

"I could die sweetly where I stand," said Ealasaid, shrunk in weariness and grieving, "but for Alan here," she added, looking at the lad beside her.

"Dying here, dying there," said Red John, "I'll dance a reel at your wedding."

He was fastening the rope round Ealasaid's waist as he spoke.

"There's one thing in my mind," he said, in some confusion of voice.

"What is that?" she asked, with small interest written in her swimming eyes.

"It's about Alan," said he (and busy about the rope): "I am your debtor for many hours I robbed you off, unthinking – my old weakness, as I told you."

"That's all bye," she said; "that's all bye and done with. Do you fancy I'm thinking now of such small sorrows? If you borrowed my lover, you pay for the loan with my life saved; I owe you that."

"I'm all the better pleased to hear you say it," said Red John, "because your taunt about my botched life rankled."

"I did you less than justice; one should never judge a life till the end of it."

Down the rock face the two men lowered her to the cave, where she let herself free of the rope, with a shake of it for her signal.

"Hurry lad," said Red John, looking into the glen; and Alan went over the edge, and down, foot and hand, eager enough to join Ealasaid.

The torn mists blew farther down the glen, the wind took a curve round Sgornoch-mor, and eye and ear told Red John that a band of the Athol men were close on him. He saw their bonnets on the slope, and heard them roar when they saw him beside the haw-tree.

"My sorrow!" said he, "here's Red John at the end of his tether! The pair below need be none the worse nor the wiser, for who's to get at them with the rope gone?"

He lifted the rope a little to make sure that Alan was off it, then slashed at it with his dirk till he cut it from the tree.

"Here's a cunning and notable end to the botched life," said the boon companion to himself, turning, with the dagger still in his hand, to face the Athol men.

And the rope in heavy coils fell past the cave mouth to the deep below.

Notes

JAUNTY JOCK
Page

1   *West Bow*   A street in Edinburgh curving down from the Lawnmarket to the Grassmarket.

1   *nine-gallon tree*   A wooden barrel containing nine gallons of ale.

1   *Luckenbooths*   A row of covered stalls which could be locked up (lucken) in the High Street of Edinburgh. They were demolished in 1817.

1   *lands*   The name given to the high tenement buildings (this one rising to 14 storeys) in the old town of Edinburgh. The poor lived in the lower and upper floors, the wealthy in the middle.

1   *emptied vessels from the flats above*   In the absence of modern plumbing it was the practice of the inhabitants of the Old Town of Edinburgh to dispose of waste by throwing it out of the window on to the street below. This action was prefaced by the cry *Gardyloo* (from the French *Gardez (vous de) l'eau* "watch out for the water".)

2   *law plea affecting the family*   The cousins have probably come to Edinburgh to have a legal dispute settled at the Court of Session, the supreme court in Scotland.

3   *seriatim... brevitatis causa* (one after another... for the sake of brevity.)   The lady's use of legal Latin immediately makes Barrisdale suspect that her father is a lawyer. He is, in fact, Lord Duthie.

3   *Barrisdale*   Jaunty Jock appears to be the nickname of Colin MacDonald of Barrisdale. The historical Barrisdale belonged to the MacDonalds of Glengarry. His home was in Barrisdale in Knoydart. He was Captain of a Watch (G. *freiceadan*) which exacted blackmail (G. *màl dubh*) or protection money from Highland chiefs and Lowland farmers to ensure that their cattle were not "lifted". His operation extended from Inverness to Flanders Moss.
Fletcher of Achallader refused to pay him blackmail, so Barrisdale stole his cattle. The Fletchers took him to the Court of Session and eventually he was imprisoned and died in jail in Edinburgh in 1737. He did not fight at Culloden, as some sources assert. (See Tearlach Coventry, Gairm 133, Glasgow, An Geamhradh 1985–6: pps 78–80.)

4   *credit ye with Latin and French*   Barrisdale also appears in Ch 8 of Neil Munro's novel *The New Road* (1914). There he is portrayed as a bombastic bully who has a thin veneer of classical learning. The hero Aeneas, however, soon punctures this and proves it to be very superficial.

4   *rough bounds* (G. *Garbh Chriochan*.)   Technically the wild country of the West

Highlands extending from Loch Sunart in the south to Loch Hourn in the north, embracing Moidart, Morar and Knoydart.

5 *Jamie*   James Francis Stuart, the "Old Pretender", father of Bonnie Prince Charlie. He was exiled in France and attempted to regain the throne for the Stuarts in 1715 with the help of the Earl of Mar. After this he spent most of his life in Rome and he died there in 1766.

5 *Crown Counsel*   The advocate (barrister) who prosecutes a case on behalf of the Crown.

5 *Appin*   This refers to Stewart of Appin. Appin in Argyllshire extends from Loch Etive in the south to Loch Leven in the north. It belonged to a branch of the Stewart clan.

5 *Glen Nant's rich daughter*   Glen Nant is in Argyllshire, stretching from Taynuilt to Kilchrenan.

6 *We'll better let that flea stick to the wall*   Idiom meaning, "We had better ignore that incident."

6 *Paisley plaid*   An expensive shawl of the famous Paisley pattern made of cashmere and wool or silk, or cotton and wool.

6 *the citadel*   Edinburgh Castle.

YOUNG PENNYMORE

10 *the Rebellion*   The Jacobite uprising of 1745 led by Prince Charles Edward Stuart. Argyll was predominantly territory of Clan Campbell, strong supporters of the Hanoverian government, and it would, therefore, be most unusual to find Jacobite supporters like John Clerk there.

10 *Pennymore*   A farm on the west shore of Loch Fyne between the villages of Kenmore and Furnace.

10 *the Duke*   Archibald, 3rd Duke of Argyll.

10 *Clonary*   (G. *Claonairigh.*) A small township on the west shore of Loch Fyne near Bridge of Douglas, south of Inveraray.

10 *(Lord) Elchies*   One of the three Law Lords before whom John Clerk was tried in the High Court of Justiciary in Inveraray.

10 *Creag-nan-caoraich* (G)   More correctly *creag-nan-caorach*, the rock of the sheep. An outcrop of rocks by Loch Fyne at the south end of Inveraray on which was erected a gallows where criminals were hanged. Now known as "The Craigs".

11 *the Lord Advocate...Prestongrange*   William Grant, Lord Prestongrange. The post of Lord Advocate was, and still is, a political appointment. In the eighteenth century he had much the same powers as the current Scottish Secretary of State. He had the authority to commute John Clerk's sentence.

11 *It was the year of...1752*   This was also the year of the notorious Appin Murder which was clearly the inspiration for this story. James Stewart of Acharn, "James of the Glen", was tried before a predjudiced Campbell jury and executed for his alleged part in the murder of Colin Campbell, the Red Fox, in the wood of Lettermore in Appin. This provides much of the subject matter for Robert Louis Stevenson's novels *Kidnapped* (1886) and *Catriona* (1893).

11 *jee his beaver*   Idiom meaning, "show any concern". Literally, "move his fur hat".

13 *behind the fair*   Idiom meaning, "too late".

13 *Gregorian Calendar* In 1752 Britain finally rejected the Julian and adopted the Gregorian Calendar to bring itself into line with the rest of Europe. The relevant Act of Parliament stated that 3rd September 1752 should become 14th September 1752, that is, eleven days were to be dropped. John Clerk was to be hanged on 5th September which now technically no longer existed, and his father naively believed that his son "could not die but on the day appointed". (p13)

15 *Kenmore* A village on the west shore of Loch Fyne south of Inveraray.

A RETURN TO NATURE

17 *Cruachan* The name of the highest mountain in Argyll. It was adopted as the war cry of Clan Campbell.

17 *since the year 1745* 1745 was the year of the Jacobite Rising led by Prince Charles Edward Stuart, known in Gaelic as *bliadhna Thearlaich* "Charles's Year".

18 *Rob Roy* Rob Roy MacGregor (1671–1734), the colourful folk hero who waged a persistent feud with the Duke of Montrose and was famous as a champion of the poor and oppressed. He is buried in Balquhidder Church Yard in Perthshire.

18 *Alasdair Dhu* Black (haired) Alasdair. *Dhu* is the conventional English rendering of the Gaelic word *dubh* (pronounced *doo*), "black".

18 *Children of the Mist* Although this name is frequently used for the MacGregors who as a clan had been outlawed and their name proscribed in 1603, Munro invariably applies it to dispossessed and homeless members of Clan Macaulay, the "true 'children of the mist', a sept of the Clan Macgregor". (Neil Munro, *The Clyde* , London 1907: p112)

21 *Cnoc Dearg* (G) Red hill.

21 *St. Kilda* Name of the most westerly Scottish island group, 40 miles west of Harris. The last inhabitants were evacuated in 1930. (There was no Saint Kilda, this name being a misunderstanding of *Skildar*, the name for the island group on an early map. Hirta is the name of the main island.)

22 *Moidart* This area between Ardnamurchan in the south and Arisaig in the north is the heartland of the MacDonalds of Clanranald.

23 *Ben Buidhe* (G) Yellow mountain.

23 *Ranald More Macaulay* (G. *Raghnall Mòr MacAmhlaidh.*) Big Ronald MacAulay.

24 *the age of Mar* John Erskine, 11th Earl of Mar (1675–1732) (nicknamed Bobbing John because of his facility to change sides), led the Jacobite Rising on behalf of James Francis Stuart, the "Old Pretender" in 1715. He was defeated at Sheriffmuir.

25 *Lammas* 1st August, a Scottish Quarter Day.

26 *Arisaig* Coastal township in South Morar, south of Mallaig and west of Fort William.

26 *keeping your place for you* Idiom meaning, "doing your work for you".

27 *durante furore* (L) While in anger.

28 *Ne dominia rerum sint incerta neve lites sint perpetuae* (L) There would be no question of uncertain ownership or unending litigation.

THE BROOCH

30 *(de) haut en bas* (F)   From top to bottom.

30 *en cabochon* (F)   Rounded on the top and flat on the back without facets.

32 *the one Book needful*   The Bible.

35 *Mahoun*   The Devil. Originally used for Mohammed who was thought in the Middle Ages to be a pagan god.

37 *the final verses of the seventh Psalm*   (*Behold, the wicked man conceives evil, and is pregnant with mischief and brings forth lies. He makes a pit, digging it out, and falls into the hole which he has made. His mischief returns upon his own head, and on his own pate his violence descends.*) Psalms 7 vv14–16. Wanlock has, of course, dug his own pit by squandering his sister's dowry.

39 *dree his weird*   Endure his own fate.

39 *Blednock brownie*   Munro may have absorbed some of the ideas for this story (1) from Galloway folklore. In William Nicolson's poem "The Brownie of Blednoch" the Brownie (Aiken-drum) is impervious to the power of the Bible like the creature in this story:

> *But the canny auld wife cam' till her breath,*
> *And she deemed the Bible might ward aff scaith,*
> *Be it benshee, bogle, ghaist or wraith –*
> *but it fear'd na Aiken-drum.*

("The Brownie of Blednoch", *Poetical Works of Willam Nicolson*, Castle Douglas, 1878. Anthologised in Hannah Aitken, *A Forgotten Heritage*, Edinburgh and London 1973:p33)

(2) more immediately from the painting "The Brownie of Blednoch" (1889) by the Kirkcudbright artist E.A. Hornel, (a friend of Munro and one of the "Glasgow Boys").

39 *a clot of the blood that dried on the spear of the Roman soldier*   A reference to the blood on the spear of the Roman soldier who pierced the side of Christ at the Crucifixion.

40 *"Though thou shouldst bray a fool in a mortar...."*   Proverbs XXVII v22.

THE FIRST-FOOT

42 *First-foot*   In Scottish tradition the first person to enter a house after midnight on Hogmanay (New Year's Eve).

42 *Flanders Moss*   The western extension of the Carse of Stirling between the Gargunnock and the Menteith Hills. It was notoriously marshy and dangerous at the time the story is set. It is now a very fertile area, having been reclaimed by eighteenth century "improving" lairds.

42 *port o'Menteith*   A village to the east of Aberfoyle.

43 *Fintry*   A village on the north side of the Campsie Fells.

44 *Kippen*   A village west of Stirling.

44 *Stirling rock*   Stirling Castle and the old town of Stirling are built on an impressive rocky eminence.

44 *Campsie lairds*   Landowners whose properties were at the foot of the Campsie Fells.

ISLE OF ILLUSION

47 *Morar* A wild and beautiful area between Arisaig in the south and Mallaig in the north.

47 *Barra Isle* Barra (with Vatersay) is the most southerly inhabited island of the Outer Hebrides.

49 *Arcady* Arcadia. A district in ancient Greece supposed to be a pastoral paradise.

49 *Bernera... Harris* Islands of the Outer Hebrides.

49 *Lochmaddy* The port of North Uist.

49 *Ealan Faoineas...Isle of Seeming...Isle of Illusion* *Faoineas* in Gaelic is, in fact, a much stronger word than Munro's translations of "Seeming" or "Illusion" would indicate. It means "vanity" or "folly" – from which the lovers have to be rescued.

50 *Barra Head ... Butt of Lewis* The southern and northern extremes of the Outer Hebrides.

51 *a priest of Eriskay* A tongue-in-cheek reference to a Catholic priest whom Neil Munro knew and admired, Fr. Allan McDonald, better known in the Hebrides as Maighstir Ailean. He was parish priest first at Dalibrog in South Uist (1884–93) and later in Eriskay (1893–1905). He was a distinguished folklorist, poet and lexicographer as well as being a devoted pastor to his people. He is the model for Fr. Ludovic in Munro's novel *Children of Tempest* (1903).

51 *"The woman tempted me, and I did eat"* See Genesis Ch3 vv12 and 13.

THE TUDOR CUP

55 *the House of Quair* Name clearly borrowed from Traquair House, also beside the Tweed and near Peebles.

55 *Ballad Minstrelsy* Walter Scott published his *Minstrelsy of the Scottish Border* in 1802–3.

58 *Meldrum* Name borrowed from Munro's friend David Storrar Meldrum, novelist and employee of William Blackwood and Sons.

61 *"The greed of English thieves brought them here marauding for good six hundred years..."* A reference to the Border reivers, many of whom of course were Scots.

"COPENHAGEN": A CHARACTER

62 *Copenhagen's school* Modelled on Glen Aray school, near Stronmagachan, founded c.1793. Munro attended it intermittently himself. The dominie, who lost his leg at the Battle of Copenhagen (1801), is perhaps partly based on the master there when Munro's mother was a pupil and partly on John MacArthur, who kept the school 1841–94.

62 *Kilmailie* Presumably Kilmalieu, the ancient graveyard of Inveraray.

63 *Nelson* "Copenhagen" would have seen Nelson during the Baltic campaign of 1801.

63 *by-name* nickname (G. *farainm*).

63 *diurnal peat* Until the Education (Scotland) Act, 1872, it was the custom in many parts of the Highlands and Islands for each schoolchild to bring a peat

each day. "The daily peat had been, for many of [the old folk], the only contribution to the cost of their children's education, except an occasional hen, a print of butter or a trapped grilse from a pot-hole in the river, which helped to furnish the dominie's larder." (Munro, *The Brave Days*, Edinburgh, 1931: p25)

64 *"cries"* The wedding banns.

65 *the Beenickie* Almost certainly the by-name of a real contemporary of Munro, possibly from G. *binneach*, "light-headed", "fanciful".

65 *"Glenorchy pint"* Whisky from an illicit still in Glenorchy.

65 *Another time – on the night of St. John's* June 24. Inveraray Masonic Lodge, St. John No.50, has its charter dated 1747. Munro belonged to it and was for a time its bard.

65 *clerk in a law office* Munro was a clerk in Inveraray in the law office of William Douglas c.1877–81.

THE SILVER DRUM

67 *Urquhart* It is very likely that the character Urquhart is partly based on Munro's friend the sculptor/poet Pittendreigh McGillivray (1856–1938). He was closely connected with the group of artists known as "The Glasgow Boys".

68 *an R.S.A.* A member of the Royal Scottish Academy, Edinburgh.

68 *Torres Vedras...Waterloo* Wellington constructed the defensive Lines of Torres Vedras in Portugal at the beginning of the Peninsular War (1808–14). Part of his army was stationed at Quatre Bras before the Battle of Waterloo, 1815. The sculptor Urquhart says that he joined the army when he was sixteen and a half. He is said to be "a man of sixty years or thereabout" (p67), thus the sittings described in the story are supposed to take place c.1852!

72 *nibble at the shilling* "Take the King's Shilling", given on enlistment in the army till 1879.

THE SCOTTISH POMPADOUR

78 *Monte Cristo* Possibly an allusion to the novel *The Count of Monte Cristo* by Alexandre Dumas père.

78 *Lucullus* L.Licinius Lucullus (c.110–57 BC), a Roman general famous for his life of luxury after retirement.

78 *Ville Lumière* Paris, "City of Light".

80 *Prevost and Chatran, Chelmonski the Napoleonic painter, Paul Delourade the poet* Alexandre Chatrian (1826–90) collaborated with E.Erkmann in writing novels. E.M. Prevost (1862–1941) was a novelist. Paul Déroulède (1846–1914) was a poet and anti-Dreyfusard.

81 *home of the exiled James of England* James Francis Stuart, the "Old Pretender" and father of Bonnie Prince Charlie, spent the earlier part of his life at St. Germain. In later life after the Jacobite defeat at Sheriffmuir he moved to Rome where he died in 1766.

82 *Tuileries* Gardens near the Louvre (Paris).

THE TALE OF THE BOON COMPANION

85 *Loch Finne* Old form of Loch Fyne.

85 *Colkitto Macdonald and his Irishry and the Athol clans* . Alasdair MacColla, died c.1647, son of Coll Ciotach MacDonald. He commanded Irish and Highland forces under the Royalist Montrose. Coming from winter quarters in Athole, they invaded Argyll in December 1644. (See Munro's novel *John Splendid* (1898).)

85 *Badenoch wolves* Badenoch is part of modern Inverness-shire, around Kingussie. Alexander Stewart, natural son of Robert II, was known as "the Wolf of Badenoch", hence presumably this phrase.

85 *Carnus* A farm-town at the head of Glen Aray, no longer occupied.

85 *Cladich* (G. *cladach*, shore). A village where the Inveraray–Dalmally road reaches Loch Awe.

85 *Knapdale* Narrow part of Argyll, between the Crinan Canal and Kintyre.

86 *Cowal* (G. *Comhal.*) The large area between the east shore of Loch Fyne and the Firth of Clyde.

86 *Carrick ditty* A song from Carrick on Loch Goil.

86 *Ealasaid* (G) Elizabeth.

86 *Coillebhraid* (G) A croft-house near Inveraray. Spelling now current is *Coillebhraghad*, "wood of the neck or throat", perhaps from the nearby small glen of *Eas a'Chosain* through which it is approached.

87 *real Argyll* Argyllshire, roughly between Loch Fyne and Loch Awe.

88 *MacCailein Mor* The Gaelic title for the Earls and, later, Dukes of Argyll. Literally, "Son of Great Colin" (the 13th-century Sir Colin Campbell of Loch Awe).

88 *Aora glen* Glen Aray. *Aora* is the Gaelic spelling.

88 *Gearran road* The road along the Gearran (G. *Gearr Abhainn*, short river). It is really the lower reaches of the River Shira (G. *Siorabh,* lasting) below the Dubh Loch.

88 *Shira glen* Glen Shira, two miles north of Inveraray. It provides the setting for many of Munro's stories.

88 *Maam, Elrigmore and Elrigbeg, Kilblane and Stuckgoy* Farm names in Glen Shira: Maam (G. *mam*) "a breast-shaped hill"; Elrigmore, "big deer trap"; Elrigbeg, "little deer trap" (G. *eileirg*, a v-shaped deer trap); Kilblaan, "church of St Blane" (G. *cille*, church); Stuckgoy, "windy pinnacle" (G. *stuc*, pinnacle, *gaoithe*, of wind)

89 *Ben Bhuidhe... Ben Shean... Tomgorm* Gaelic names of hills at the head of Glen Shira: *Beinn Bhuidhe*, "yellow mountain"; *Beinn an t-Sithein*, "mountain of the fairy hillock"; *Tomgorm*, "green knoll".

89 *Sgornoch-mor* A great steep slope strewn with rocks or scree.

89 *Stacan* (G. *Allt an Stacain*), "burn of the little steep hill or cliff" rises near the head of Glen Shira and flows west into Loch Awe.

89 *the home of the reiver* Presumably an allusion to Rob Roy MacGregor, whom the 2nd Duke of Argyll allowed to live in Glen Shira for seven years. The site of his house is still marked on maps.

Glossary

Abbreviations
(G) denotes Gaelic, (S) denotes Scots Language, (F) denotes French, (L) denotes Latin.

airt (S)	direction
airting (S)	moving in a certain direction
anchorite	hermit
bardachd (G)	poetry
beiking (S)	basking, warming itself
bellwether	warning (*literally* the leading sheep of a flock which had a bell hung round its neck)
ben (S)	inside
bibelot (F)	knick-knack
bickering	flowing swiftly and noisily
bided (S)	remained
bien (S)	(pronounced *been*) comfortable
birchen shaws(S)	birch woods
bittern	a marsh bird of the heron family
blackmail (S)	originally payment exacted in return for protection against the plundering of cattle and other livestock (G. *màl* rent, *dubh* black)
blate (S)	shy, diffident
bogle (S)	ghost
bombazine	corded fabric of silk and worsted
bonnet-laird (S)	small landowner
boon	merry, kind
bouillon (F)	broth
boutonnière (F)	button hole
bray (in a mortar)	grind into small pieces
brevitatis causa (L)	for the sake of brevity
brioche (F)	soft loaf or roll
broadcloth	fine woollen fulled black cloth i.e. respectable clothes
buidseachas (G)	witchcraft
burgess	citizen of a burgh, town dweller
by-name	nickname (*G. farainm*)
cabar (G)	rafter
cabinet	apartment

cadger	pedlar, hawker
canaille (F)	rabble
canorous	resonant
cantrip (S)	trick
carle (S)	fellow
cat-a-mountain	wild mountain animal e.g. leopard, panther
cateran	Highland robber (*G. ceatharn*)
ceilidh (G)	visit
chamade (F)	drum roll call for a parley or surrender
chopin (S)	Scottish measure : approximately a half pint
cicerone (Italian)	guide
clachan (G)	village
claymore	large two-edged sword (*G. claidheamh mòr*)
close (S)	narrow alleyway
corrie	hollow between mountains (*G. coire*)
coulisse(F)	wing (of a theatre)
coxcomb	fool
cozen	deceive
creach (G)	plunder, usually cattle
crenel	notch in a parapet
crepitation	crackling sound
cuaran (G)	moccasin
dandiacal	foppish
darach (G)	oak
denominate	specific
Dhia (G).	God (*nominative : Dia*)
divot (S)	piece of turf, sod
Dod (S)	God (euphemistic imprecation)
doomster	the court official whose duty it was to pronounce the sentence on a convicted criminal as directed by the judge
dour (S)	humourless
droll	funny
dryad	wood nymph
dunny (S)	cellar (contraction of *dungeon*)
durante furore (L)	while in anger
ealan (G)	island (usual spelling *eilean*)
eas (G)	waterfall
egret	a plume (*F. aigrette*)
en cabochon (F)	rounded on top and flat on back without facets
factor	manager of a chief's estate
faoineas (G)	vanity, trifling
farceur (F)	joker, buffoon
fash (S)	trouble yourself, bother
ferrule	more correctly *ferule* : a cane used for punishment
forbye (S)	besides
fresh-caumed (S)	recently whitened with pipe clay

gangrel (S)	tramp, vagrant
gawk (S)	awkward, clumsy person
geumnaich (G)	lowing of cattle
gey (S)	very
girning (S)	(1)snarling (2)grinning
gled (S)	hawk
gommeaux (F)	properly *gommeux* : toffs , fops
goodman (S)	head of the household, owner of the house
grew (S)	quake with horror
haar (S)	a sea mist
hag (S)	hollow in marshy ground
halbert	a long shafted axe-like weapon with a hook on its back
(de) haut en bas (F)	from top to bottom
hautbois (F)	oboe
Hielan(d) (S)	Highland
Jew's Harp	a small musical instrument played against the teeth by plucking a metal tongue
jyle (S)	jail
kail (S)	broth usually made from curly cabbage
ken (S)	know
kenspeckle (S)	conspicuous
kent (S)	knew
kist (S)	chest
kyloe (S)	one of a breed of small Highland cattle (from *G. gaidhealach*, Gaelic, Highland)
lalland (S)	Lowland
Lammas (S)	1st August
land (S)	tenement house
lanthorn (S)	lantern
lawing (S)	tavern bill
lifting	stealing, plundering (from *G. togail*, lifting)
linn	pool (*G. linne*)
(on) list	at the customer's pleasure
loof (S)	palm of the hand
Luckenbooth (S)	a booth or covered stall which could be locked up
lugger	small boat with a square sail
macconba	snuff
maun (S)	must
mirk (S)	dark, gloomy
mo thruagh (G)	my wretchedness! woe is me!
mochree	my heart, my darling (*G. mo chridhe*)
mufti	the civilian dress of a soldier
nine-gallon tree	a wooden barrel containing nine gallons of ale
ower (S)	over, too
parterre	flower bed
patten	wooden shoe

pend close (S)	arched passageway
pennyland (S)	originally an area of land for which the rental was a penny
Petronella	a Scottish country dance attributed to the fiddler Nathaniel Gow
pibroch	pipe tune (G. *piobaireachd*)
plack (S)	a coin of small value
poignard	dagger
polity	system of government
poltroon	coward
powney (S)	pony
precentor (S)	a person appointed to lead the singing of the congregation line by line
premiss	presupposition
premonstration	warning
Psalmody	singing of the Psalms
pyot (S)	magpie
rale (S)	real
ran-dan	carousing
rattan	cane
redoubt	retreat
reel-rall	(into) a state of confusion
reiver (S)	plunderer, raider
reveille (F)	drum call at daybreak to waken the soldiers
risp (S)	a piece of metal (also called a 'tirling pin') against which a metal ring was rubbed to produce a high grating sound. Equivalent of a modern door-bell.
roe	species of small deer
roulade (F)	embellishment
rouse	reveille
sapple (S)	froth, lather
saugh (S)	willow
scale stair(S)	straight (as opposed to spiral) staircase
screen (S)	shawl, headscarf
scrug	tug over the brow
sennachie	story teller (G. *seanachaidh*)
seriatim (L)	one after another
shelister	yellow iris (G. *seilisdeir*)
sheuch (S)	ditch
shieling (S)	high summer pasture usually with huts for the herdsmen
skliffin' (S)	shuffling
soothfast	reliable
spang (S)	stride out
speaking-trumpet	an instrument for making the voice heard at a distance, a megaphone
surtout	overcoat
swound	swoon, faint

tacksman (S)	a chief tenant who sublets his land to lesser tenants
tambouring	embroidery
tattoo	drum beat calling soldiers to their quarters
teind (to hell) (S)	tithe (to the Devil)
thrapple (S)	throat
tithe	tax, levy
togail (G)	lifting, plundering
tryst (S)	market, fair
umber	brown
unco (S)	awful
virginals	spinet (old keyboard instrument)
wae (S)	grieved, sorrowful, loath
warrandice (S)	guarantee
waulking-wicker (S)	frame for drying fulled cloth
wraprascal	loose greatcoat
writer (S)	lawyer
wynd (S)	narrow street, lane

The Works of Neil Munro

Short Story Collections

The Lost Pibroch and Other Sheiling Stories, William Blackwood, Edinburgh, 1896
Ayrshire Idylls, (With illustrations by George Houston), Adam and Charles Black, London, 1912
Jaunty Jock and Other Stories, William Blackwood, Edinburgh, 1918
The Lost Pibroch, Jaunty Jock, Ayrshire Idylls, Inveraray Edition, William Blackwood, Edinburgh, 1935 (This edition contains the additional story "Ius Primae Noctis" in *The Lost Pibroch* collection.)
The Lost Pibroch and Other Sheiling Stories (With introduction and notes by Ronnie Renton, Rennie McOwan and Rae MacGregor), House of Lochar, Colonsay, 1996.

Novels

John Splendid, William Blackwood, Edinburgh, 1898
Gilian the Dreamer, William Blackwood, Edinburgh, 1899
Doom Castle, William Blackwood, Edinburgh, 1901
The Shoes of Fortune, William Blackwood, Edinburgh, 1901
Children of Tempest, William Blackwood, Edinburgh, 1903
The Daft Days, William Blackwood, Edinburgh, 1907
Fancy Farm, William Blackwood, Edinburgh, 1910
The New Road, William Blackwood, Edinburgh, 1914
The New Road (With introduction by Brian D. Osborne), B & W Publishing, Edinburgh, 1994
John Splendid (With introduction by Brian D. Osborne), B & W Publishing, Edinburgh 1994
Doom Castle, (With introduction by Brian D. Osborne), B & W Publishing, Edinburgh, 1996

Travelogue

The Clyde, River and Firth (With illustrations by Mary Y. and J. Young Hunter), Adam and Charles Black, London, 1907

Humorous Sketches

Erchie, My Droll Friend, William Blackwood, Edinburgh, 1904
The Vital Spark, William Blackwood, Edinburgh, 1906
In Highland Harbours with Para Handy, William Blackwood, Edinburgh, 1911

Jimmy Swan the Joy Traveller, William Blackwood, Edinburgh, 1917
Hurricane Jack of the Vital Spark, William Blackwood, Edinburgh, 1923
Para Handy (Complete edition with introduction and notes by Brian Osborne and Ronald Armstrong), Birlinn, Edinburgh, 1992
Erchie and Jimmy Swan, (Complete edition with introduction and notes by Brian D. Osborne and Ronald Armstrong), Birlinn, Edinburgh, 1993

History

The History of the Royal Bank of Scotland 1727–1927,(privately printed) Edinburgh, 1928

Poetry

The Poetry of Neil Munro (Collected and with preface by John Buchan), William Blackwood, Edinburgh, 1931

Journalism

The Brave Days (Selected and with introduction by George Blake), The Porpoise Press, Edinburgh, 1933
The Looker On (Selected and with introduction by George Blake), The Porpoise Press. Edinburgh,1933